Fear the Night

Sean Bunce

Fear the Night

Vanguard Press

VANGUARD PAPERBACK

A CIP catalogue record for this title is available from the British Library.

ISBN 978-1-80016-558-8

Vanguard Press is an imprint of
Pegasus Elliot Mackenzie Publishers Ltd.
www.pegasuspublishers.com
First Published in 2023

Vanguard Press
Sheraton House Castle Park
Cambridge England

Printed & Bound in Great Britain

To my father. For everything.

Note from the Author

When I was thirteen years old, I awoke one night to find a figure sitting on my window sill that resembled the shape of a large man. Although I found out the first night that this 'man' was only in the dream world version of my room, his presence still terrifies me to this day. I'm twenty-nine now, and throughout the past fifteen years of my life, I've had several encounters with this dream entity. Each experience has been different, evolving based on how I responded to the most recent encounter. Sometimes, I'm paralyzed and aware of what's happening, and other times, I'm not aware that I'm in the dream until I'm being pulled off my feet. The more I encounter it, the more it evolves to the point where I now believe it's separate from me entirely. Over the years, the frequency of these dreams has also decreased, giving me the feeling that the entity waits until my guard is down until it will strike again. The only issue is — I don't know how to keep my guard up.

This story is based on my encounters with this 'unnamed man'. So far, I haven't been able to do so much as face my dreams, fearing the time when he'll come back. This is an attempt to not only face him, but conquer my fear. Maybe doing it through fiction will help me do it in the dream world as well. So far, nothing else has worked.

This story takes place during my college years when my contact with the entity was most frequent.

Prologue:
FROM THE BEGINNING

I

The first time I saw him, he was sitting on the bench near my window. His broad shoulders and head were covered in what looked like a hooded cloak. Half of his body stayed immersed in the shadow, from my closet, while the other half of his outline is illuminated by the street light outside my window. ,

Lying on my side in the fetal position, I clung to the blankets around me. All I could do was stare, unable to consider anything else. I dared not move for fear of the worst. As hard as I tried, I couldn't force myself to pull the blankets tighter around me. The bench where he sat was no more than an arm's reach from my exposed foot. I wanted with every fiber of my being to pull my foot in. How long I stayed that way, I do not know. The longer I did, however, the more my heart felt like it was in a vice, squeezing tighter with every attempt to move. Soon, all I could imagine were the terrible things that might happen if I couldn't escape.

In agony, I began to question if I even had the courage to reach for the light switch just behind me. A commentary began in my head. Would he reach me before I turned on the light, the voice in my head asked, analyzing the probability without landing on a solid answer.

When I woke up the next morning, I couldn't remember how I escaped the man in my room, and I wondered if it was real or just a bad dream. Scanning the room, my eyes lock on the he bench near my window which is empty except for my backpack sitting in the same spot I saw the figure. I lay there, staring at that spot, wondering, if it was just my backpack the whole time.

I thought about it for a while, attempting to convince myself that it was just a backpack the and that I wouldn't to experience this nightmare ever again. it wasn't real, then why did I feel so afraid?

The very next night, it was difficult to fall asleep. I first lay down at nine p.m., but kept the light on until nearly midnight when my eyes started to become heavy.

The light was on when I opened my eyes again.

Sitting in the same corner, the hooded figure made no attempt to move. the shadow cast from his hood made it difficult to see any facial features underneath. This time, the man was leaning towards me. His elbows resting on his knees and his pale, slender fingers interlocked.

The familiar cool liquid trickled down my spine.

With each passing breath, I felt as though I'd never have another. I was trapped. As much as I attempted to move, my body wouldn't listen. No more than three feet from the back of my head, was the door handle. As my thoughts turned toward it, my heart raced faster and faster. Could I reach it? I wasn't sure. For what seemed an eternity, I debated the small move that would take so much courage. My dad was just down the hall on the other side of the door. I knew I could make it if I ran, but all I wanted was to hide under my covers — to wait until he left. the he sat there, watching me under his dark hood, I did nothing, once again.

I carried the guilt from these encounters with me for the next two years, waiting anxiously for the hooded figure to show up.

II

For a few years — maybe two or three — I didn't have any more of these dreams. More importantly, I never saw the man in the hood. When I was seventeen, my father and I moved to Hailey, Idaho, a small, mountainous town, connected to three others — Ketchum, Sun Valley and Bellevue. The whole valley consisted of just over eleven thousand people. The house we lived in, was a two story, three bedroom town home. The house was a far cry from the trailer we moved from . It was also closer to where my dad worked and where I went to school.

During the time my father and I lived at that house, my younger brother and sister often stayed the night. By this, I mean every other weekend. Their room connected to mine through a bathroom that doubled as a hallway when my siblings were feeling lazy, and I hadn't locked the door to my side.

And of course, I didn't lock it this time.

Although I wasn't aware of what time it was, I hoped when I opened my eyes that I would still have a few more hours to sleep before my alarm went off. It was Saturday, however, and I never set my alarm on weekends. It was also too dark to be morning.

As I lay in bed with my back toward the bathroom, I heard the distinct sound of footsteps walking toward me on the fake wood floor of the bathroom.

Then I hear a voice.

"Little boy," the voice whispered. "Little boy, wake up."

As the footsteps grew louder, so too did the harsh voice. "Little boy, wake up," the voice commanded. "Little boy, wake up and play with me." The voice went quiet as it neared, and soon, so did the footsteps.

He's standing over me, I thought to myself.

I tightened the grip on my blanket, trying my best not to be caught moving. I felt the person's breath on the back of my neck, which sent a chill down my spine. The voice was angry now. I could almost feel his gritted teeth as he spoke quietly, trying not to wake up the rest of my sleeping family.

"*LITTLE BOY, WAKE UP*," he whispered loudly, sitting down on the bed behind me. The weight of his body on my bed created an indent that felt more like a black hole pulling me closer as it grew. His hand moved to my shoulder, shaking me gently at first and then harder as the seconds passed.

"LITTLE BOY, LITTLE BOY, LITTLE BOY, LITTLE BOY!" The man's voice grew faster and faster as he shook me, reminding me of my little brother when he wanted to annoy me. Then it stopped. The shaking. The voice. It all stopped.

I felt him waiting.

The silence gripped my spine painfully as I waited for what I felt might be the end.

Suddenly, I felt the weight lift off my bed. There was still no noise except for the relief exhaled from the springs in my mattress.

The voice spoke again.

"Fine," it said. "I'll go play with your brother and sister."

At this moment, I found the courage to move. I threw my right arm back over my shoulder. My fist clenched around the edge of my blanket, I aimed to strike the person behind the voice. As I turned, the only thing I hit was air. My eyes caught the edge of what I thought was a cape as it disappeared into the bathroom. I got out of bed and ran after the voice until I was in my siblings' room. The room was empty except for my brother and sister sleeping soundly. I walked out into the main hallway just above the stairs, turning on light switches to illuminate the stairway and small hallway.

The living room downstairs remained dark, casting an eerie shadow across the landing at the bottom of the stairs. Another shot of pain gripped my spine as I realized I must go down there, eventually.

Although I was sure my dad's room was safe, I checked it anyway, opening his door silently and tiptoeing in to make sure the man hadn't snuck in to hide. When I turned to head out of his room, I took a glance at my dad, only half remembering that he had been sleeping. His snoring assured me that I hadn't disturbed him.

I shut all three upstairs doors after grabbing my small flip phone to use as a light. As I walked down the stairs, I realized that it wouldn't do anything to split the darkness. Instead, I felt as though it would only be a beacon for my position in the dark, should anyone be waiting. I kept it open anyway, mostly as an omen of hope. If the stairway light went out, it might be able to give me some visibility. At least more than my own eyes.

I took my time, tiptoeing down the stairs, listening for a sound. Any sound. I was held up by the fact that my phone light turned off every fifteen seconds without use, requiring me to press a button that let off an audible tone each time, like a psychotic version of Marco Polo in the dark. Even the volume buttons made a tone with each level I turned it down until finally, it was quiet again.

My only hope was to make it as far down the stairs as possible before the light went out, which terrified me greatly. In the moments of temporary darkness when the flip phone went out, the intruder would have his chance to pounce.

Reaching the bottom of the stairs came as both a relief and a silent curse. I would now be revealing whatever hid in the vast darkness of the living room, and

I didn't have a weapon. What was I thinking not waking my dad up when I was up there, I thought to myself. Regardless of the fear I felt, I couldn't let the intruder get away.

I flipped the light switch on, blinding myself from the transition from dark to light. A moment later, after my eyes adjusted, I peered around the banister, scanning from the front of the living room to the kitchen in the back of the house. I walked through the room, turning on lamps to expose any shadows that might hide someone. I made my way to the kitchen — nothing. The back sliding door was still locked. Cautiously, I checked the downstairs bathroom after grabbing a large cutting knife on my way through the kitchen. I opened the door leading to the garage, the light from the kitchen hallway spilling into more vast darkness before I flipped on another blinding light switch.

Nothing.

I carried the knife to my bedroom, leaving on all the lights in my house as I walked back upstairs — a subject my dad would scold me for in the morning, but that was the morning. I wasn't able to get any more sleep by the time my scolding came; the intruder made sure of that. Until the next morning, I sat on the edge of my bed watching TV with the door to the hallway open, kitchen knife and my metal Louisville slugger next to me on my bed to keep me company.

III

When I was nineteen, I went to college in Coos Bay, Oregon. A rainy, coastal town, it wasn't a good fit for a baseball team. Nor a baseball player largely uninterested in baseball at the time. I was an undersized, fifth-string catcher on a junior college team that essentially seemed like a stepping stone for major league athletes. Even at six foot two and a hundred and eighty pounds, I was the smallest one on the team, and it showed. I was used to being the best, so the idea that I was the bottom man of an entire team startled me. Not humbled. I used my status as a player to get girls — a lot of girls. My cool reputation didn't change the fact that I would be cut from the team halfway through the semester. Or that I wouldn't return for the second semester, but spend a month on my friend's couch in Albany doing much of the same.

On one occasion, I decided to try my luck at getting with a girl on campus I often saw doing laundry. She was a beautiful girl, with long brown hair and green eyes; she also liked scary movies but didn't fall for my 'Would you like to watch one at my place' routine that usually led to other things. Instead, we watched the first *Paranormal Activity* at the theatre (before I knew it was fake).

Afterwards, she went back to her dorm with a kiss on the lips and a promise for coffee in the morning that would ultimately be canceled, both because I wasn't looking for longer than a one night effort, and because the next morning I felt like shit.

As I lay down for bed that night, I turned on the TV, mostly to watch, but also as a form of night light. As cool as I thought I was, I was still afraid of the dark, for good reason.

Around one a.m., the movie on TV broke to a commercial for OxyClean and a guy with a bearish beard selling me his product in a commanding voice. I shifted a little in bed to get lower on my pillow. With my blankets around my chest and arm over my covers, I began to feel uncomfortable, as if a presence stood just behind me in the space between the small closet of my dorm room and the headboard of my bed. Before I willed myself to move, I was pulled by my shoulders into my closet, the darkness closing in all around me. I shook my head violently, watching in slow motion as my dirty, white socks disappeared into the dark void. When I opened my eyes again, I was awake. My arms were in the same position as before — over the top of my blankets. The same commercial played on the TV — the man with the bearish beard, still talking about his wondrous product. Sitting up in bed, I turned so that my back was toward the cement wall. With the light on, I watched the closet the rest of the night with an endless string of infomercials playing in the background.

Fear The Night

Chapter I

As I lie on my stomach, hands tucked neatly under my deflated cotton pillow, I struggle to remember how long I've been awake. My eyes try their best to adjust to the dark room. Out of the haze, I identify the large, oak dresser only a foot from the edge of my bed. Two dark rectangles on the walls across from me slowly become doorways leading to an oversized living room and kitchen. The calm silence that typically fills the morning air is interrupted only by the raging glow of the neon-red alarm clock inaudibly clicking another minute past two forty a.m.

A drop of sweat begins to slowly roll down my forehead, and with it, the familiar feeling of an itch that needs to be scratched. As my eyes adjust, I begin to see through the two large doors in my room leading to the spaces of my house. I think about this feeling for some time, letting the urge to wipe the sweat away sink in until I'm unable to tolerate it any longer. Before I start to move my hand from underneath me, however, I hear a loud thud on the roof above me. I'm startled at first, but then my cloudy brain begins to grasp for answers as to what it might have been. Before I'm able to make a connection, another booming thud hits the top of my roof. Then another. With the third loud thud, a calm starts to stretch itself over me like water slowly creeping along the base of a bathtub. I feel it first at my toes, and as the cool feeling reaches my spine, I become aware of what it is making the noise. I attempt to move my hands to push myself up to a sitting position.

Nothing happens.

I hear another large thud on my roof and another, until the sounds begin to resemble footsteps walking toward the back door next to the kitchen. From my confined view, I can see through the kitchen hallway. The kitchen is too dark to make anything out. I try again to move. The feeling of water running over me is replaced with the heavy weight of lead now resting on my back and arms, keeping me pinned down. Helpless. I begin to panic, reaching with everything I have for the edge of the bed. The steps on the roof speed up with each attempt to move as if the person responsible for them is aware of my presence. My mind reaches as well, to the memory of an eighth grade wrestling match when I reached for the edge of the mat, saving myself from being pinned. After grabbing the mat and pulling both of us out of bounds I was able to get a restart and take him down for the win.

Not this time.

This time, my arms can’t reach the edge of the mat because the opponent won’t let me.

The footsteps stop above my back door.

Chapter II

Though the dreams still scare me and leave me afraid to go back to sleep, at this point in my life, twenty-four years old, I have developed a way of 'shaking them off'. Whenever I sense that I'm in a dream, I immediately shake my head and make myself wake up. This always hurts and leaves a lasting headache, but it's the only way I've found to avoid the dreams.

Despite my fear of going back to sleep, I need it. The last five days, I've seen very little of it between work and school. Not only do I have an early calculus exam at ten a.m., but I also work afterward until six at night.

Three thirty a.m.

I lie on my stomach once more. This time, I keep a large hunting knife under my pillow, only inches from my open hand. Just in case. Though it's been some time since I remember closing my eyes to fall back asleep, my eyes are open again and I wonder why. At first, a cool, calm feeling flows over me as if I've just gotten a good night's rest, but somehow in the back of my mind I don't believe it. And then another feeling rushes over me.

My heart begins to quicken until it is nearly beating out of my chest. My spine is stiff, preventing me from moving. I begin to panic, feeling like I'm trapped in a box and can't breathe.

Staring through the still darkness, I'm suddenly aware of another person in my small house. There's still no sound, but I know someone's here. I sense the weight of the knife just outside my fingertips, the impression it creates in my pillow above my knuckles. As much as I want to move my hand the few inches for the smooth handle of the ten-inch blade, nothing happens.

In all my struggles to reach the short distance, I forget to listen for movement coming from other parts of my small house. This stops me.

I think to myself, was there movement?

I can't remember. I have to reach for the knife. I try again, this time with all the strength my body will allow, knowing that in my struggle I won't be able to hear the movement of the man in my home.

Seconds feel like hours as I will my hand forward, grabbing the knife. All at once, I'm able to move to a sitting position. I move quickly to the light switch across my room, hoping I am the only one moving through the dark. As a blinding flash of light drowns out the darkness in my room, I look around frantically. Both doors leading to my room are open, with the living room and kitchen still pitch black.

As the minutes pass, I remain with my back to the wall, listening for any movement and holding the large knife for comfort. I don't know if I have it in me to use it, but the feeling of the cold steel in my hand erases any doubts I might have.

"This is a waiting game now," I whisper to myself, too terrified to move any further than I have. I think about closing the doors, but there are no locks on the handles.

As minutes fade into hours, my eyes become too heavy to lift any more and I fall asleep leaning against my bedroom wall, the large knife clutched in my hand as it rests on the floor.

Chapter III

The dream is immediate. The light in my room is still on and although the large, neon numbers on my clock continue to click a few minutes past six in the morning, I find myself unable to really comprehend time or what it means as the numbers continue to change, minute after minute. What I am aware of is the feeling, yet again, that I'm not alone in my own home. I'm both frustrated that I fell asleep waiting, but also afraid that the person in my house could have done just about anything while I was passed out.

As I begin to call out, taunting the unknown person, large footsteps, quick and heavy, run across the floor of my kitchen and start on the short hallway just before my open bedroom door. With my back still against the wall, I try to move away and turn to face the charging stranger, but I'm unable to do so. I look down at my right hand where the knife lies waiting, but my fingers won't close around it. I feel hopeless. As the weight of the person's presence bears down on me, I close my eyes, waiting for the blow that never comes.

When I open my eyes again, I'm still in my room, lying with my back against the wall.

It is 6.29 a.m.

This time, I don't have the feeling that someone's in my house. I'm able to move my hand holding the knife, but I'm still careful as I check my house, turning on each light as I cautiously enter each room.

Satisfied that my house is empty, I decide it's best not to fall back asleep no matter how much I need it. I switch on the TV in the living room and turn to SportsCenter for the morning highlights. There isn't much going on in the world of sports, but it's still something to take my mind off the night's events.

At times, I welcome normal nightmares — the ones where something might be chasing you, or your boss decides you need to scrub the toilets, or even the occasional nightmare about a popular scary movie — but these are different. In a way, they leave a tiny scar upon my soul, one that often bleeds when I think of my past experiences with the man in my dreams. Each new scar opens the wound a little more, reminding me about the other times, growing the fear that I feel with each new experience — the fear of the dark, of sleep, of seeing the person who torments me in my dreams. While I'm awake, I often catch myself thinking about how utterly helpless I feel.

Never before have I been stuck so long on the same terrible nightmare, and the more my eyes grow heavy, the more I fear it will happen again.

Around eight thirty a.m., my head nods back on the couch, and as my jaw loses its fight with gravity, a loud snore echoes throughout my well-lit house.

Chapter IV

From the kitchen, I hear the clickity-clack of hooves walking on the linoleum floor. I turn my head toward the direction of the noise and see an animal moving toward me, its four long legs moving one after the other in an uninterested fashion. Although I'm not able to identify the name for this animal, the word for it is just on the tip of my tongue. As the large animal approaches me, it begins a slow turn until it's facing the kitchen. With no more than a glance back at me from its left eye, it starts walking back from where it came.

Without thinking much about the situation, I stand up and follow the animal into the kitchen, the name on my tongue pulling me forward. The urge to say its name is so strong, I'm unable to let this creature out of my sight.

Before I'm able to decide what to call it, however, the animal is gone, and the name 'llama' saturates my tongue like the leftover taste of garlic. In the llama's place is a man I feel I've met before. The man standing before me has a large, round face. His hair, which only grows around the outside of his head in a crown, reminds me oddly of Kevin from the TV show The Office, or my friend Waldo from student media.

Paul ‘Waldo’ Waldonowski was given his nickname for his propensity to get lost when drinking with his friends. This always led to a small manhunt throughout the downtown bars. He’d typically be found passed out next to a pizza joint or on his way home, stumbling drunk.

At first, I feel nothing for the man in front of me — not hate, nor fear. We stare at each other unblinking for what seems like a long time before it dawns on me who this might be. As a connection begins to form in my mind, I see a faint smile emerge on his face until it stretches nearly to his ears. Suddenly, I know the man in front of me. This time, he isn’t wearing his hood.

On the stove, a pot of boiling water is raging with triumph that it’s finally reached maximum temperature. How it got there, I’m not sure. Before another thought enters my head, I grab it. Turning the handle sideways, I shove the open end of the pot towards the man standing before me. The scalding water strikes him in the face. For a moment, I almost feel like I’ve won. This feeling is quickly replaced. The hot liquid continues to steam as it rolls down the man’s smiling face. His wide eyes remain open the entire time, revealing not even the tiniest flinch.

I decide I’m done watching this man’s display of strength, so I quickly shake my head, bringing me back to my couch, late for my test.

Chapter V

Running out my front door in one of my red sweatshirts, a pair of sweatpants and running shoes, I'm nearly half a block down the road before I realize that I might not have locked my door. I glance down at my watch — 10.03. I'm three minutes late for my test already. No time to go back. I'm not overly worried about my house getting broken into anyway; the neighbors next door are illegal immigrants who never come outside except for work, and the three girls across the street are hippies who always spend their mid-afternoons outside doing yoga or yard work. One of them, a blue-eyed blonde, shouts, "Good morning," as I pass. I don't have time for much of a hello as I sprint by, but I send a meager wave in her direction.

It has been a few years since high school sports and the half semester of failed college athletics, but I've managed to keep relatively in shape. Still, I can't help but stop running a half mile after I started. Two blocks past Beacon, I turn onto University Drive, hoping to see a shuttle bus along the street to pick me up. There isn't one. Continuing to jog, I tuck my thumbs under the straps of my backpack, empty except for my journalism notepad, a pencil, and a copy of *The Gunslinger* by Stephen King that I picked up in a thrift store downtown. The book is about a knight of sorts, wandering through the desert trying to chase down a mysterious man in black. A good book, but it is only the first in the series and I'm not sure if I am willing or able to devote such a great amount of time to that sort of a cause.

Entering the seven-story education building at 10.17 a.m., I slow my jog to a fast walk as a crowd of students meets me trying to exit in the opposite direction. I reach the two building elevators in time to catch one closing, full of kids. The other one's door also begins its slow, methodical slide shut. I catch the eye of a blonde-haired girl whose face says, "Too late, sorry," and "I'm glad it wasn't me."

Turning right, I go through a door indicating the stairwell laid behind it, one I admittedly didn't use until times like these, even if I had a class on the second floor.

Reaching the fourth floor, I exit the stairwell, sweat pouring down my face. Three classrooms down the hall on the right I come to a stop, taking in one deep, calming breath to make sure I don't sound as though I've just run from home. It doesn't work, however, as I'm still breathing hard when I enter the quiet classroom. My teacher, Mr Randall, is sitting behind his desk as I walk over, and doesn't look up as I grab a large packet from his desk. He obviously knows who has entered twenty-two minutes late.

"I'm glad you could make it, Mr Harrison," Mr Randall says in a half-hearted, insincere tone. "The test will be over at eleven fifteen." A fact I already know, but the way he says it sounds as if he's taunting me, knowing I might not finish.

Mr Randall was a short, round man, who often had shiny red skin that reminded me of some of the hardest drinkers I'd seen at the school. There wasn't any hiding behind his square-rimmed glasses. Even a blush wouldn't have shown that red against his otherwise pale white skin. Nor would the glasses hide his absolute disdain for being here to teach such uninterested students.

"Thanks," I say, with an equally insincere tone, knowing I have a shot in hell at finishing. I hate that he calls me Mr Harrison. It always sounds awkward to hear someone address me by my last name. Especially when they knew my name was Elliot.

I take the only open seat near the front of the class and next to a beautiful, brown-eyed girl, too focused to notice anyone sitting down late next to her. I open the packet and turn to the back, looking at how many problems my Kool-Aid-faced teacher assigned for the test. *Fifty!*

Chapter VI

The test goes by in a long, terrible blur. My sunken, bloodshot eyes attempt to focus, only picking up bits and pieces of each problem. Luckily, most of the questions are multiple choice. At the start of question ten, I look at the clock on the wall behind the teacher. Its hands make the only audible sounds in the room other than the scratching of pencils on paper. Ten fifty. Twenty-five minutes left. I know that I might not finish, which stresses me out, but it also takes my mind off the previous night. For that I'm grateful.

For the next twenty-five minutes I struggle Toward the end, I start guessing, circling answers to the last ten questions without really looking at the problems. I look up in time to see the clock's hands move to eleven fifteen.

"Tests in," Mr Randall says, still looking down at the papers on his desk. He appears to be marking answers on someone's test with almost the same speed as I had answered the last few problems.

As I place my test in the basket to the left of Mr Randall on his desk, I can't help but notice a tiny smirk on his face as his red pen happily slashes across the paper in front of it. He's enjoying this, I think. This must be his favorite part.

Chapter VII

After exiting the classroom as one of the last ones to finish my test, my mind finally has a chance to slow down. When it does, I long for the fast pace in which my morning started. Walking down the hallway, I enter the elevator next to a guy who's shared most of my classes since freshman year. He too is apparently interested in getting an easy degree in communication. Nate, I think his name is, but I can't remember. I hardly noticed him asking how I felt about the test.

Instead, my mind dwells on the fear induced from the night before, each nightmare burning into the back of my brain. I can hardly recall the last normal dream I had, Because Those never seemed to leave a lasting impression. Yet, it doesn't take any effort at all to remember the way I felt last night while a stranger walked around my house. Or the way I felt the first time he sat in the window sill in my room. The memories of those nightmares often feel more like real memories than many of the events that have occurred in my life.

Noticing that I might not have heard him, Nate asks me, "How do you think you did on the test?" this time speaking a little louder.

"Oh," I say, acknowledging the person next to me in the elevator for the first time. "Probably not so well," I admit. "I studied last night, but I couldn't sleep very much, so I pretty much just guessed most of the time." As I turn my head to look at the person standing next to me, I notice he's dressed in a similar-looking outfit — sweatpants and a sweatshirt but also a blue, flat-brimmed baseball hat with a white Los Angeles Dodgers logo on the front. His brown hair pokes out from the side in different lengths and his beard hasn't been trimmed in at least a month. But he looks more confident about the test now that someone has clearly done worse.

"Yeah, there were a few I had to guess on too," he says. "I feel like he purposely puts in equations that we haven't worked on."

"Probably," I say. The way Mr Randall was smiling as I placed my test in the box, Nate is probably right.

I don't say anything the rest of the ride on the elevator and the conversation turns to an awkward silence. When the elevator door opens, Nate exits first, eager to get away. I follow soon behind, lost in thought once again.

Chapter VIII

The walk across campus is a slow one as I drag my feet, trying my best to shake the images that now scar the backs of my eyelids. It was always this way after. The fear. The anxiety. The constant flashbacks to the image of my friend Waldo, only slightly more inflated, like a balloon, wearing a smile that continues to chill my bones.

In a moment I would be at work, a small student newspaper called The Arbiter, where I'm the assistant news editor, making just a hundred dollars a week. Not enough for the amount of work I put in, but writing is my passion, and I was only too happy to take the job before last summer. Before I realized how poor I'd be once the job actually started and had to take out more loans. I would have to see my friend Waldo, who also works at The Arbiter as the assistant sports editor. Monday and Wednesday were always press days, which meant there was a deadline that couldn't be met and too many unfinished articles to fix, edit, verify, then cut some more because the information couldn't be verified and the article couldn't be pushed again. "Not again, Elliot," I could hear my unorganized, scatterbrained co-editor Hannah Cross saying already. And stress, lots of stress. Today was no exception. Later, we would all get a beer at a dive bar off campus and reminisce proudly about how we adapted to our challenges of the day and overcame them, more or less without ripping each other's heads off.

As I walk into the office, clearly at the wrong time, our editor-in-chief, Stephanie Parker, walks swiftly from the small back space occupied by the design crew to her desk without so much as a glance in my direction. Her face is bright red, like most days, from frustration. Her shoulder-length, curly blonde hair bounces behind her and her oversized, olive-green high heels clack on the floor as she stomps by. Stephanie always wore clothes that clashed, like the thinly strapped yellow and white-flower summer dress she has on today, which exposes her atrophied-looking legs about five inches above her knee.

The rest of the room seems to be steaming with frustration as well, which often happens. The room is separated into four sections — the editorial section consists of two editors each for news, sports and culture. The design, marketing, and business team all have their own separate cubicle areas. When one group feels stressed, it often spreads like a cough, passed on by those who walk between the cubicles. Like Stephanie, every print day. She has a knack for it, and as much as we try to defend ourselves against the oncoming anxiety of the day, it never really works. We snowball, one after the other. Luckily, I'm one of the last ones to enter the office and have no idea why everyone is in such a panic. I really don't want to know either.

I sit down at my desk, expecting an onslaught of work from Hannah, who always seems to be in the weeds when we organize stories onto our designated pages. Hannah has frizzled, brown hair and bangs that are always too long. At certain points in the semester, she breaks down from fits of anxiety and curls up under her desk, a place many of us wind up, either from late night writing, drinking, or both, when there is a stressful story to write for the next morning's deadline. To hide her from passersby, or from my own sight sometimes, I build Hannah a fort under her desk with a large office beanbag chair and a small blanket I keep on the back of my chair. At least today hadn't gone that bad by the time I opened my laptop at eleven forty.

Chapter IX

"What's got you down?" Hannah asks, noticing that after ten minutes of sitting next to her I haven't said hello. The bags under my eyes are also a clear indication that I haven't slept.

Hannah, as much as she often came off as a space cadet, was also the most caring person in the office. As much as we argued, we also shared a good friendship and a few too many beers on occasion.

Being the space cadet that she is, however, she neglects to remove the earbuds snugly placed in her ears, giving her voice an amplified tone as if she is talking in a loud room. But she isn't, and from the desk directly behind Hannah and me, I hear the voice I wanted to avoid as long as possible. I'm not sure what will happen if I see the long smile stretched across my friend's face.

"Hey, buddy, how are you today? Are you feeling all right?" Waldo asks, his voice moving closer behind me with the sound of his desk chair and his large frame rolling across the thin carpet.

"Just tired," I say, still not looking away from my laptop. "I didn't sleep last night and I'm pretty sure I just failed my math test." I leave out the part about my nightmares seeming to be so real that I'm now afraid to go to sleep. The bags under my eyes will surely be worse by tomorrow if I'm unable to find a way to sleep. There will be no hiding it then.

Despite our lack of any real paycheck from student media, the meager wages each week did allow for one thing every journalist seems to need at some point — coffee. The three of us hardly needed an excuse to walk across the street three to four times a day, which always helped to eat away at our paycheck, but kept us going when our bodies or our minds couldn't. More than once already this semester, each of us found ourselves working through a full on burn-out due to the amount of work we needed to do for the paper and school. Nearly every time, our solution, good or bad, was to walk the short distance across University Road to the coffee shop in the Student Union building and get the most caffeine we could fit in a cup. If this didn't work, we would repeat the process, adding a couple shots of caffeine until our brains kicked on, and deciding to work again. Sometimes it didn't work, but deadlines are deadlines, so we killed ourselves getting our work done.

The worst thing in the world, even worse than death, was not making a deadline. This wasn't because the paper would fail; we have plenty of advertisements to fill space, but because other writers in the office would mark it in their memory and bring it up at the worst time, like in the middle of an argument or important meeting. I would say people were petty for this, but in this environment, you grasp at any thread that blows in the wind and hope their shirt unravels so you can get a promotion and not them. Anything to get an ounce of praise or a chance at the editor-in-chief job next year.

I order a large, black coffee with three sugars and four shots of extra caffeine. The short, dark-haired girl taking my order, as nice as she is, seems to have her own sleep issues. The bags under her eyes are the first sign. It becomes more obvious when she gives the people ahead of us the wrong order.

"Large black coffee with sugar and extra shots," I reiterate, trying not to sound like I'm micromanaging her. I hope the taste of coffee will do enough to wake me up, but if not, the extra kick might. Most days I feel as though gears in my body are spinning, but their teeth, ground off long ago, offer no traction. Instead, they just spin in place, providing no power to other bodily systems.

After months of twice-a-week deadlines, sometimes publishing three to four articles a week, it was understandable that at this point in the semester we all felt no different than the machines used to print out the papers we created — barely seeing what went on the page, but knowing it was permanently printed on thousands of papers.

Chapter X

Later in the evening, after a long day editing pages and doing anything I can to take my mind off Waldo's inflated, zipper-like smile, I slowly walk the two miles home to the tiny pink corner lot. As I turn the final corner, just a block away from my front door, my feet start to scuff the ground as if they're trying to slow down on their own and a sudden anxiety knots my stomach.

Although it's dark, the street light outside my house casts a shadow on the door, stretching further than normal, it seems to me. As I near the foot of the steps leading up to my door, I feel it sink deeper and deeper into the shadow of the awning. This feeling continues until it begins to pull me in. All at once, I feel several invisible hands on my back, pushing me toward the awaiting mouth of the door. The only protest audible comes from the scuffs of my shoes on the cement just before the welcome mat. In the back of my mind, I can hear the turn of a key in the lock, but my mind is too tired to process the connection to my hands, and I feel as though I'm floating.

My only desire is to lie down, to close my eyes and fall asleep.

Chapter XI

Sleep could have come easy tonight, like turning off a light switch. Instead, I decided to fight it, turning the thermostat down to sixty-five degrees in my already cold home. I then fill my coffee pot as full as it will go before scooping five large spoonsful of Folgers coffee into the small, white filter. "Extra strength," I say out loud to myself for reassurance.

Tonight, I planned to finish assignments for class, work on articles for the paper, or if I needed to, play another career of *Madden 2009*. The game is outdated, but it's more than enough to occupy my time. Anything to stay awake and avoid seeing the wide-grinned man again.

After I drink the first half of the thirty-two-ounce thermos of coffee, I start to feel the ground-down gears inside my chest spin. At this moment, I realize the most terrifying thing — no amount of coffee can save me. Eventually, I'll fall asleep. If not tonight, then tomorrow night or the next, but eventually sleep would come, and the dreams that came with it.

An online search tells me that I might be able to make it eight to ten days without sleep before I die. I certainly don't plan to take it that far. Hallucinations would come around three days. I decide this will be how long I'll go before trying to fall asleep again. If I can make it that far.

I hope to find a solution, or at least a little courage before then.

But first, I will have to make it through the night.

Chapter XII

Including the prior night, I can count on one hand how many hours I've slept the last two days. Throughout the night, an invisible battle rages within my chest as though a candle struggles to repel the darkness that sleep would bring. As much as the coffee provided fuel to the tiny fire burning inside me, I feel myself nod off more and more until the short, blonde whiskers on my chin touch the bare skin of my chest. The first time this happens, I'm startled awake, scratching the itch under my chin while looking around my living room for the person responsible. After I sit back on the couch, assured that I am safe, I never feel the warning of the tiny whiskers again.

At six thirty a.m., I stand up from the couch, stretching all six foot two inches of my tall frame; my joints announce their disapproval with a loud crack. I let out a yawn that reminds me of an elk call I once heard, hunting with my dad. My darkened, sunken eyes half open, my feet scuff the carpet with each step as I walk to the bathroom, touching each wall for cautionary support along the way. The water in the shower never reaches much above room temperature on most days, something I've gotten used to over the past couple months living in this house. Because of this lack of hot water, a morning shower often takes no more than ten minutes. Much of this time is spent away from the water with one arm wrapped tight to my chest while the other scrubs quickly. This morning, however, I welcome the shock the cold water presents as it does more to wake me up than anything else. I welcome the shivering also, standing with my face open to a steady stream from the neck-high showerhead.

Class didn't begin until eight thirty, and although I don't have much work left after the all-night binge, I relish any excuse to leave my house at a somewhat normal hour. I would spend the two hours before Art History in the library, where the thought of sleep might be less tempting. In my hundred-person Art History class, however, it might be a little more difficult. My tendency, even with a full night's rest, is to find the seat closest to the heater vent and take a morning nap. I can't do that today.

The walk to the library passes by in nothing more than a haze as my exhaustion sets in more than ever. The blue, thirty-two-ounce mug in my hand is emptied on the way and filled again at the Starbucks just outside the library. The encounter is so much of a blur that I hardly realize the change in taste of my coffee. Two sips into my second large thermos, I can no longer feel the gears in my chest spinning in futile protest. The feeling is soon replaced by desperation to fall anywhere and shut my eyes. I begin to daydream about the comfort I would feel if I only stopped for a second at one of the couches I see on the way through the library.

The front desk attendant, a short, wide-eyed girl barely taller than the counter she stands behind, offers a friendly hello as I pass by without acknowledging her. The library seems unusually empty for this hour of the morning, I think to myself as I look down at my cell phone for the time. In the few seconds I'm focusing on the screen, I nearly run into an island of computers used to search for books. I see the blurry, black computers in the outline of my vision, and like I did so many times in high school, I spin away from them to my left. Unlike in high school, when I was agile and fully awake, my spin move only makes things worse. My right foot catches the back of my left as I begin to turn, making me fall to the ground face first. My left hand, holding the cell phone, hits the ground at the same time as my right holding the large coffee mug (with a tight lid, thankfully). Although the cell phone falls out of my hands, the coffee doesn't spill a drop.

Standing up embarrassed, I walk towards the way I fell without looking to see who saw. A short way down the hall, I press the elevator button, waiting for the door's long, slow slide open. Everything takes more time when you're embarrassed. The only thing keeping my mind in the fight at this point is the fear of what might happen if I give in to temptation and fall asleep, and what dreams will come if I do.

Hitting the button to the fourth floor, I wait for the doors to close and the elevator to begin rising. The top floor of the building would be the last to be filled so early in the morning, making it the best place to play loud music. When I make it to the top floor, I exit and walk toward a small conference room with a large window that always makes me feel like a fish in a bowl. Entering the room, I make myself comfortable, setting my backpack down beside the large office table and my coffee mug on top. I pull my laptop out of its bag, open it, and turn it on.

Sitting down at the desk, I feel the exhaustion wash over me like a bucket of water dumped on my head. First, my eyes begin to close slowly while I wait for the laptop screen to load. I shake my head and chug a few large gulps of coffee, attempting to shrug off the oncoming sleep. The internet browser finally loads with Pandora radio on its home page. The first step to a good study session is always choosing a good playlist.

My eyelids grow heavy again. This time, I let them shut all the way, soaking in comfort for a few seconds. It feels so good to finally relax, I think to myself.

For a moment, I feel safe. The fear of falling asleep is gone. But in the still silence, I hear a voice call from far away. At first, I couldn't hear what the voice was saying. It sounds muffled. Then, as if the person calling yelled it in my ear, I hear the message, "Wake up!"

I sit up abruptly, slapping my cheek and looking around to see if there is anyone in my small room. The browser is still open on Pandora, so I select a playlist from the list on the screen: 'Classic Rock'.

I open another window on my screen and begin looking through my class's website to see if there is any work that I can do. From the unseen screen, a recognizable sound begins to echo throughout the small room. Although one of my favorite songs, my foggy brain can't think of the name. Its soothing beat does nothing to help me keep my eyes open. Within minutes, I am fully asleep. Both my arms submit, crossing underneath my head as I lay it down, eyes sewn shut. A voice calls from a distance, but it's too quiet to hear.

The song continues to echo from the laptop.

Chapter XIII

As I sleep, with my forehead firmly planted on the desk in front of me, the clock on the wall in the small space continues to click away the time — one hour first, then another, and another. When I finally wake, my head is shifted, facing the clock on the wall to my right.

10.22 a.m.

Upon seeing this, sheer panic sets in. Trying my best to stand up and run out of the room, I think to myself how I can explain to my teacher that I am not absent for the seventh time and she doesn't need to fail me outright. Instead, my head remains pinned, facing away from the door and toward the clock on the wall. The seconds continue to tick away without mercy. My hands are trapped in my lap, stuck together as if at prayer.

From the other side of the door, I hear shouting between two people, though most of the conversation sounds like it is coming from under water. A few times the two people talking say my name, but the rest is too muffled to make out.

Just a moment after the conversation between the two strangers ends, I hear one walk away and the other, standing silently at the entrance to the door, speaks loud enough that I can hear him through the thick wood. "Is it okay if I come in?" the voice asks. I recognized it immediately.

I try as hard as I can to scream the words, "No you can't!" but the room remains silent.

My head is still firmly planted on the table facing the clock on the wall. I hear the door behind me open and someone begins walking slowly toward my back. As the person passes by my seat, I try my best to look toward his face, but I'm only able to make out a blurred peripheral view of his upper torso. He sits down across from me, his body resting so softly in the chair that I strain my ear to hear what chair he's taken. I feel him place his hands upon the table and for a moment I wonder how they can feel so heavy. He wants me to know he has the power, I think to myself. For a while, nothing is said. The air feels thick with tension, and I can feel the fear slithering up my right leg like a snake.

"By this time, you're probably realizing you have nowhere to run," the man says in a calm, businesslike tone. "How long did you make it, two days? I've seen better."

Another pause.

I struggle to respond. The words are like peanut butter in my mouth.

"Don't bother responding," he says, brushing away my attempt to speak with a wave of his right hand. "This is more of an informational visit. No questions necessary." He seemed to be enjoying himself at this point. "I typically have this visit around the time that people begin to fight their sleep cycle. You see, it's not good for you to miss so much sleep, buddy. The last guy nearly scrambled his eggs on the sidewalk outside his apartment building doing that."

As he speaks, a question forms in my head. "Why does it matter if I die?"

"Good question, Elliot. You see, it doesn't really matter to me if you live or die to be honest with you. I guess it's really your choice; if you keep pushing yourself and not sleeping, I'm going to make sure your hallucinations drive you mad. If you go to sleep like a good little boy each night, I'll continue to visit you every once in a while to make sure you're doing all right. You know, mentally."

With that, he pushes hard away from the table and stands across from me.

"It would be too easy for me to squash your head on this table and end this little game of ours." I feel his cold eyes piercing the top of my skull as he weighs his options thoughtfully. Laughing as he walks past my paralyzed body, he opens the door, pausing with one hand on the handle. "If you fall asleep tonight, like a good boy, I'll know you accept my deal. If you don't, well…"

Without another word, I hear the door close behind him.

Chapter XIV

I wake with a start, violently pushing myself away from the library desk and realizing all at once that he was right; I can't run. As I bend down to pick up my bag, the blood rushing to my head nearly makes me pass out. I look at the clock on the wall after standing.

8.05 a.m.

I have plenty of time to get to class, I think aloud.

I leave the library and begin walking toward class, the man's words echoing in my head. With each echo, a shot of pain reverberates through my brain. With each ping sent coursing through my head, I'm forced to forget any thoughts I have from my encounter. Instead, I'm left with a single question gnawing at the back of my mind — do I have enough courage?

One way or another, I know that I need a plan for tonight. If I hold out, by day three I can expect to start hallucinating. If I make it longer, I might lose my mind. Option 'A' was never really an option. I've lived in those days of allowing him access to my mind and the fear that he loves so much. Away from my dreams, I feel confident enough to outlast the unnamed man, but as the minutes tick by on my watch, doubt begins to creep in.

Chapter XV

I arrive at class just two minutes before it's supposed to start, and luckily, I'm able to find a seat at the back of the large auditorium-style classroom. Although I've never really paid attention in this class when I have been present, I've still seemed to do all right cramming last minute to pass each test. As far as entry level classes go, this one is probably the easiest.

The study guide our professor gave us for each test is always pretty much the real thing with a different name; a fact most people figured out early. Most people, like myself, never came back until test day because of this.

I guess a few times no one showed up at all, so the professor started taking attendance and emailed us all to let us know. 'Due to lack of attendance during lectures this semester, I will now be taking down names that are not present. If you are receiving this email, you have missed the maximum allowed days. Your next absence will result in your unenrollment from the course.'

I don't care much about failing, especially considering I have other things on my mind now, but the course is too easy for me not to show up and take the grade. It turns out a few others in the class have the same mindset. The back row fills quickly after I sit down.

I remember an entry level psychology course I'd taken freshman year, mostly to meet girls. During one of the lessons I actually took interest in, I remember the professor talking about lucid dreaming. It might not have been part of the lesson, though, because I don't remember seeing it on any test. I definitely don't remember what the teacher said about it, but it is the only thing I remember from the course, so I look it up to see if it can help me.

It doesn't take long to find results after I type the letters 'lu' into the search tab, the first thing that pops onto the page is 'how to lucid dream'. It must be a popular search.

Within less than a minute, I have what I need.

Lucid dreaming — to become aware of the fact that you are in a dream. By getting better at recognizing certain qualities in a dream that are different from reality, the dreamer can eventually take control of elements within the dream.

With more time, the process of lucid dreaming becomes easier, I read.

That was my first problem — time. My second issue was that in order to practice lucid dreaming, I had to sleep. Most research about lucid dreaming suggested that I keep a dream journal and begin focusing on signs that I'm dreaming. For a person to get used to lucid dreaming, it would typically take more than one night. I had today, and that was it. Part of me wondered if I could sleep tonight and tolerate my first visit from my tormentor. That thought quickly vanished when I remembered all the other interactions we had in the past. Still, a strange hope remained — that somehow, I might be able to control my actions in the dream world and find a way to fight back before it is too late.

The most important part of preparation for lucid dreaming is to be able to recognize the dream world from the real. To do this is simple, I just needed to ask myself throughout the day 'Am I dreaming?' and either push a finger through the palm of my hand or look at my hands several times after looking away. If I am able to push my finger through my hand or if my hands look different, then I am dreaming. After reading this, I am immediately reminded of the movie *Inception* and the totem pieces each person carried through the dream world. At this, I laugh. I hadn't taken the movie seriously at the time, but I was thinking now that a totem would be a good idea. Until I found one, I plan to practice looking at my hands.

Chapter XVI

Class is over quickly, but a look at my watch tells me we are out at the regular time. I take my time finishing my research before packing up my stuff. By the time I leave the classroom, I am the last one remaining. Even the professor has left without me noticing.

Walking across campus toward the student media building, I try to remember if I have any articles due for the paper this week. The walk, which normally took five minutes, takes me fifteen after stopping at the convenience store on campus to grab an energy drink. I typically never buy energy drinks, but I need it today. I also don't want to go into the office where I know I will see my coworker Waldo. His wretched smile is still stained in my memory.

If anyone is in the office, I don't notice as I walk through the maze of bluish-gray cubicles toward my desk. As I sit down, I pull my laptop from my backpack and set it on the table. I turn around in my chair to make sure no one else is in my immediate area. When I am sure I am alone, I turn back toward my desk and look at my hands. Now is as good a time as any to practice my lucid dreaming techniques.

"Am I dreaming?" I mutter silently. As I do this, I visualize pushing my right index finger through my left palm. When I am unsuccessful at pushing it through, I mutter the question again, "Am I dreaming?"

For now, I am still awake.

I search through my calendar notebook for my next assignment and see that I have one due the next day on the school's crosswalk policy. In the last three weeks, a handful of students on bikes have been struck by vehicles as they enter crosswalks on campus. Cyclists blame the drivers for not stopping soon enough or seeing the cyclists, and drivers blame the cyclists for racing across the street without looking. I have already interviewed campus security for their 'very serious' depiction of how much of an epidemic this issue is campus wide.

Three days ago, I was also lucky enough to see one of these collisions first hand. My interview with the cyclist was a little less straightforward. The cyclist was at first livid that he hadn't been given the right of way despite his late arrival to the intersection. "He should have seen me coming down the sidewalk," the rider said. Upon realizing that he was just hit by a car, and that it was probably his fault, the rider got back on his bike with a hop and raced off again before he could get his name in the paper or receive a citation from campus security. His front tire wobbled violently as he pedaled away.

I remember thinking he wouldn't be too difficult to track down.

I put my earphones in right before the front door to the office opens with another student coming in after class. It's Hannah, my fellow news editor. I say hello, looking up only slightly from my laptop to exchange eye contact. I don't remove my headphones, hoping she will think I'm too busy to talk. Hannah doesn't take the hint, and I find myself pulling out the headphone from my left ear so that I can hear her and respond while keeping my attention on my computer screen.

"So, I was thinking we run the food waste article instead of the 'how to' section this week. We're running behind on both, but the waste article is almost finished," she says. "What do you think?"

"Isn't the 'how to' just a list of steps? Why couldn't that go? I thought we had that section because it was super easy for days like this where we don't have content?" I ask in a sarcastic tone.

"Well, the problem is that I was responsible for both this week, and I only just started on the waste article," Hannah says apologetically, her face reddening

This sort of thing always happens with one of us every week. Most times, we just run an extra advertisement in our paper or another easy 'how to' guide. Running a twice-weekly paper is a difficult task when the entire staff go to class full time. We compromise and decide to run the waste story while putting in an extra advertisement to use up space.

Several of our writers also turned in rough drafts that we are nearly finished editing.

While we talk, the newsroom begins filling up. Soon, the familiar buzz of typing and conversation drowns out all the quiet from before. Putting the headphone back in my ear, the low buzz quickly transforms into the steady beat of drums and a guitar. I don't recognize the song, but I am grateful it was next on the playlist.

I finish my article on crosswalk safety around one thirty and edit our staff writers' stories until two thirty.

I begin packing up and make my way to the front of the office. I have one more class at three before I can go home. Hoping I can make it out before any other conversations spark up, I start to leave. This turns out to be wishful thinking. On my way out the door, Waldo, tall enough to see over the cubicle walls, catches sight of me from the middle of the maze of cubicles and shouts across the room, "Wait up, bro!" has class at the same time as I do most days and always walks with me on the way.

This time, it is difficult to make eye contact without thinking of the man in my dreams. To reassure myself that it isn't him, I go through my routine before he makes it within earshot. "Am I dreaming?" I whisper under my breath, turning my hands from facing toward the ground to where I can see my palms and then back toward the ground.

“I’m sorry, dude,” Waldo says, thinking I was talking about him. “If you want to walk alone, you totally can.”

“Oh, no. No worries at all. I was just wrapped up in a story I’m writing,” I lie. “I wasn’t trying to ditch you, man.”

For the next five minutes, we talk about the story I am writing on crosswalks. A few times, I nearly bring up the other topic on my mind. Waldo is a good friend, but the deeper I get into thinking about my situation, the less I want to talk about it with him. I don’t think anyone would be able to help me, and I think it would be even worse if I told my story and no one believed me. Besides, what could anyone do to help me in my dreams? I might feel even more helpless if someone knew about my issue but didn’t have the power to help me.

Parting ways as I enter the twenty-story education building at the end of campus, I briefly notice a confused and somewhat hurt look on Waldo’s face as I wave goodbye. Waldo often thinks another person’s bad day is his fault somehow or another. With me not speaking much the whole walk, I know he is kicking himself wondering why. I just have too much on my mind to let him know it isn’t his fault. Although, in a way, you can say it is.

Chapter XVII

'Reporting Public Affairs' is an interesting enough class to keep my thoughts preoccupied for an hour. Throughout the lecture, I think about the impending night only once. The more I focus on the future, the less I am able to formulate a workable plan. At this point, I can't make up my mind between the two choices — stay up all night and eventually hallucinate until I go insane or go to sleep and face whatever fear and pain waits for me.

For much of the late afternoon, it feels as though I am checking off items on a final bucket list. I was only given a day to make my decision, and whatever way my thoughts went, it felt like all roads lead to more of the same. At this point, am I really in control? Is it even a choice? Or does he already know what decision I will make? The worst part is not knowing what thoughts are shared with the person inhabiting my subconscious and which thoughts aren't. In the dream, I tried my best to ask a question, but the man answered before my lips moved. Was this proof that he knew my thoughts or a neat parlor trick?

For dinner, I walk to the grocery store across the street and buy a nine-dollar ribeye steak, potatoes and asparagus. I clean up my house, take clothes to the laundromat and even do the dishes that normally sit in my sink for a week or two. Through the whole process, I wonder if this would be my last time falling asleep

Although cleaning my house and eating an expensive (to me) meal seemed like I was preparing myself for death row, somewhere in the recesses of my mind I still have hope that I will see the next morning. I was a little shaky on the details of how that would happen, however. Every few hours, I remember to go through my routine — asking if I am still dreaming while attempting to push a finger through my palm. While pushing my finger into my palm on my last attempt, a glimpse of the face of my watch reminds me of what I'd read earlier that day — to check my awareness in a dream, I could either look at my hands as the unchanging item or the face of a clock. By looking at either hand of the clock a few times, I would be able to determine if what was happening was real based on whether or not the time changed drastically. What better totem could I have than my watch?

For the totem to work, I would need to know it well. I had worn this watch for nearly a year and realized now that I hadn't really taken a good look at it. It was always just a tool on my wrist. I take my watch off and study it. The face of the watch, black with white, glow-in-the-dark hands and numbers, has a white scratch running from the eight up the left side of the glass face to the eleven. The band is also black and shows no sign of cracking or creasing where the watch typically clasped.

By ten p.m., the fear of the impending night was enough to keep me awake. I had come to a decision. Instead of choosing either option, I would go with the hybrid of the two — staying awake (if I could) to bide my time and prepare, and when the hallucinations got bad enough, I would sleep.

I would fight.

Chapter XVIII

I make it until three in the morning before I start to feel the slightest bit tired. Since I don't have much homework and all my work is done for the paper, the only thing I can think of doing to stay busy is to play video games. My old Xbox 360, a white relic turned brown from years of collecting dust, whirrs loudly under my TV, laboring from another hour of computing data. My favorite game right now is *Call of Duty: Modern Warfare 2*. For the most part, it's not too challenging; you run around a small map shooting at other online players until the time runs out. As you get better and level up, you are also able to upgrade your weapons and what your character looks like. Level seventy is the highest you can reach for this game. If, at any point, you reach level seventy, you can start back at level one with a symbol above your name signifying that you have prestige or that you have elected to start your progression over. I have only reached prestige twice in my video game career, and it was a drag. Usually, you can achieve this by devoting a few months of your life. Apparently, I had enough. In just five or so hours, I manage to reach prestige for a third time, and by three thirty, I am bored running around in circles.

Modern Warfare was released in 2009. Now, three years later, it is still popular online and more popular still for its story mode. Essentially, the game's storyline centers around an all-out war between Russia and the United States. Russia somehow makes it to U.S. soil and it's my job to help win the war as part of a small team. As I play, the next few hours fly by.

Four o'clock comes and goes without me noticing. A quick glance at my watch every few hours, coupled with the question I continue asking myself each time ("Am I awake?"), sets my mind at ease.

Earlier this evening, I stocked up on soda, energy drinks and plenty of snacks to last until the morning. If I can make it until eight a.m. without falling asleep, I will be okay for today, I think. Class is at eight thirty, and production day at the paper usually takes all day, so I have no worries about falling asleep until I get home in the afternoon. Of course, I know I am only putting a Band-Aid on a much larger wound. For now, however, my momentary happiness is worth whatever happens later.

At seven a.m., I begin cleaning up the mess from my long night. In total, I drank ten cans of Pepsi and three Red Bull energy drinks, and ate nearly all the snacks I'd purchased the night before, including — two bags of chips, a bag of licorice, and half a bag of trail mix. Much of this I don't remember consuming, but my stomach feels different, complaining almost immediately after I begin moving around. A sour, sugary taste creeps its way out of my throat in the form of a burp soon followed by a touch of acid reflux.

Chapter XIX

As I make the walk across the busy street to campus, I begin noticing a lull in my thinking, almost like the lag of a video game experiencing bad internet connection. I knew it would be a difficult day running off no sleep, and this is one of the reasons why. I try thinking about my schedule beyond the two responsibilities I have for the day, but the gears in my thought process won't budge. After the slightest effort to think, my mind feels strained and confused.

"Am I awake?" I ask myself with another glance at my watch. 8.04 a.m. I look away and back down at my wrist. 8.04 a.m. Still awake. At this point, the act of checking my watch (totem) and reciting the same phrase is a habit no less than breathing or walking. This task, in all its simplicity, hits me with a shot of confidence and excitement, cutting through the fog surrounding my brain. It feels like a shot of espresso without the coffee to water it down. The added energy doesn't stick around, however, and I find myself standing at the back of a long line that I don't remember entering. It's as if my senses led me here without telling me where they were going.

I am the last to sit down in my Literature Analysis class, which means I get the seat in the middle of the front row of the class. No one ever sits in this seat if they can help it. I immediately realize why. The entire class period, the professor stares straight at my forehead. I am the only one she looks at while she gives instructions. This distracts me to the point where I barely hear her ask about the progress of our paper due the following day.

"We have a paper due tomorrow?" I think, without realizing the words are coming out of my mouth. Most of the class laugh. I catch a glance of the girl's face sitting to my right. She seems embarrassed to be sitting next to me as she quickly covers the left side of her face with her hand, turning away. The teacher gives no response, continuing without pause.

"Your papers will be submitted through email by this time tomorrow," she says without dropping her gaze from my forehead. "Work turned in after one p.m. tomorrow will not be graded."

I'm not sure if I've started my paper, and if I have, I can't remember the topic I chose to write about. With all that had happened the last few days, something was bound to slip through the cracks. y grade isn't so hot in this class already, and I doubt if it can survive another big hit, like a missing paper.

Without much more talking, we are released from class to finish writing our papers. Even though I probably haven't started writing mine, I don't feel too bad about it after watching a girl, who probably forgot to write hers also, sprint across campus until she disappears into the library a good two hundred yards down the walkway ahead of me. I'm going there also, but I'm not in a hurry. I had already made up my mind that it would be an all-nighter before I got to class. At least now I have something to do.

I work in the library for an hour before I need to start walking to the student media building. Tomorrow is another production day, so for today, I plan to finish articles that we need for the next edition. Our paper goes to the stands on Mondays and Wednesdays. Most of what we write about deals with campus events or information about clubs. Very rarely do we have a story that I think is interesting. It comes with the territory, I guess, and explains perfectly why no one ever reads our paper. That coupled with a generation of students who receive their news from Facebook doesn't help our pickup rates. Most students probably don't know what paper is used for, other than its most obvious uses — fire starter, packaging material and absorbing liquids.

I remember a party that I attended when I first started at student media last year. I was proud of myself after working hard on an article and having it published on the cover of the paper. When I saw a stack of maybe twenty papers on the counter of the person's house, all with my story on the cover, I was even more proud of my accomplishment. That was until I realized there were no paper towels in the house, or towels, or anything else available for soaking up spilled liquids. When someone puked in the kitchen, a handful of papers were grabbed from the top of the stack and laid out on the tile floor to prevent the spread of the watery vomit. The same thing was done when a person spilled a drink or made any other mess. By the end of the night, I figured someone had read the paper between cleaning and lying face down on the many magazines now stuck to the floors and walls of the house.

Despite our lack of an audience, most of us at the paper hold firmly to our idealistic notions that our jobs mean something if just one person reads our story. If that one person reads my article, and they become more informed about a topic, then I've done my job. Our campus readership hovers around seven hundred and fifty for each story online — not bad for a school of more than twenty thousand people, but not where we want it either.

Unfortunately, not many journalists on our staff are as outgoing as I am. One reporter from the culture section of the paper, who I never really liked, had never done an in-person interview with a source, ever. He relied entirely on email and text message conversations. For any aspiring journalist, this was a red flag. Most of us were taught not to use email because it gave your reader a feeling of disconnection from the story. When you interview a person live, you get emotion and often more information than you asked for. One of my favorite 'tricks' is to ask the person I'm interviewing a question and then remain silent for as long as possible afterward. The silence is unbearable for the other person, and makes most people start talking more because they think they haven't quite answered my question correctly.

We finish laying out the paper by mid-afternoon, and by three p.m. the consistent buzz of conversation and typing begins to die down. It is now broken up by the sound of laptops shutting, zippers zipping, and the shuffling of feet of people heading back to class. Although I finished my tasks for the day about an hour earlier, I stay in the office and work on my paper that is due the next day.

My topic is simple, analyze another author's analysis of the book *As I Lay Dying,* by William Faulkner. Simple for someone. *As I Lay Dying* is probably the most confusing book I've ever had to think about. Although this is a book I can actually say I've read, it wasn't what I expected. The story centers around a dead grandmother who is at first laid on the kitchen table while her family goes through the grieving process, standing around her. Each chapter of the book is a different character's perspective. The confusing part, for me, is that when I was reading a character's perspective, I only got their thoughts and what they saw. When characters in the book spoke, it was in another character's chapter as they saw them.

As my professor tried her best to explain, Faulkner wrote this novel in a type of writing called 'stream of consciousness'. I didn't understand what this was until about page forty of the book when the characters started moving around in the scene. In this type of novel, the plot was secondary to the reactions and personalities of the characters portrayed. Their reaction to each situation seemed to be the focus and all that mattered.

Chapter XX

It would be both awkward and crazy-looking to keep repeating the same question to myself while others are in the office. So, when I think everyone is gone, I go through the process as I practiced, "Am I dreaming?" I ask myself while looking at the time. 4.47 a.m. I look away and back again. 4.47 a.m.

"Why did you ask yourself that, man?" Waldo is sitting behind me, still at his desk. I didn't look around before doing my ritual and now I feel a small amount of embarrassment for not checking.

"No reason," I say, which isn't enough to keep him from prying further.

"Have you been avoiding me?" he asks. The hurt in his voice is audible.

I haven't turned around yet, but at this, I spin in my chair to face him. Waldo and I are usually good friends, and I have clearly been avoiding him but not because of anything he has done. I don't know how to explain this to him, however.

"I'm sorry," I say sincerely. "Honestly, I've had a lot on my mind, and I haven't been able to get much sleep."

"Yeah, I was going to tell you that you don't look very well today," he says, sounding concerned. "Are you getting sick?"

"No, I'm not," I say without continuing. We are drawing closer to the topic of my dreams, which I don't want to discuss, but I don't have the energy nor the cognitive power to come up with a good lie. After a long pause in which neither of us say anything, I begin telling him the story of the man who haunts my dreams. I leave no detail untold, including the part where the man appeared with Waldo's face at the end of a long night of frightening dreams.

Waldo seems confused by all this. His eyebrows pinch toward the brim of his nose from the strain of concentration. When he finally speaks, it is with much more understanding than I anticipate.

"That must be awful, man," he says. "Is he always in your dreams? Does it ever hurt?"

I can tell that I've sparked an interest in my friend. With each question I answer, another one takes its place. Many of Waldo's questions I haven't asked myself. My relationship with the man in my dreams has been more of a 'run first, ask questions later' sort of thing. One of the questions he asks stays with me, however, "Does it ever hurt?" To this point, the answer is no. Not once in any of my dreams has the figure caused physical harm. What he does is instill fear down to my very core — fear of the unknown and fear that… The ending to this sentence eludes me. What am I afraid of? Death? Was that possible in the dream world? Or is it that he comes when I'm not prepared? Like a scene in a movie that makes you jump even though it's not scary.

I think back to each time I have encountered the man, and there was only one time, really, when I felt like I was being grabbed from my bed. After this dream, however, I was in bed safe and unharmed. All other times I can remember, the fear from waking up and realizing I was in a nightmare was enough to paralyze me and keep me from going anywhere.

Slowly, like a pool of liquid running across an open floor, an idea begins to creep its way from the dark fog of my thought process.

"What is your schedule like later?" I ask Waldo. "I need a favor from you."

Chapter XXI

I'm tired enough now that every blink provides an extra shot of dopamine. It's as if my brain is trying to trick itself into falling asleep. Each time my eyelids close, I hold them shut just a little longer, trying to hold on to that pleasant feeling.

"Am I dreaming?" I ask myself, going through my routine. Six thirty.

Right after I finish, Waldo answers. "You're not, but I'm flattered you think I'm dreamy." He laughs nervously.

I'm lying on one of the hard-backed, wooden-armed couches in the office meeting room, with Waldo sitting next to me like a shrink diagnosing his patient.

"One hour, thirty-five minutes. That's all I'm asking for. No more," I say, setting a timer on my phone. I am the most serious I have ever been with Waldo.

I have decided it is time for me to go to sleep and practice lucid dreaming while I at least have someone to wake me up. Waldo and I have agreed that if, at any point, I start showing signs of distress (twitching, screaming, etc.), he will shake me until I wake. The final resort for me not waking is a cleaning bucket filled with cold water sitting near my head. I will enter the REM (rapid eye movement) part of the sleep cycle ninety minutes after closing my eyes, and I don't want too much time to wander around — just enough to test a new hypothesis I have and recharge my batteries.

As I close my eyes, I feel my nerves tighten with anxiety. I begin reciting another phrase I learned to help with lucid dreaming. "I will know that I'm dreaming. I will know that I'm dreaming. I will know that I'm dreaming. I will..."

Chapter XXII

When I open my eyes again, I feel fresh. I'm lying on the hard-backed couch, but Waldo is gone. The chair he was sitting in before is turned toward the door as if he made a quick exit. A strange wave of air moves over my body and suddenly, I realize I'm dreaming. I try moving my arm to look at my watch, but nothing happens. I am stuck in the spider's web. Typically, when this happens, I shake my head violently until I wake myself. But this time, I have a goal. I focus all my energy on my arms, and like a patient going through rehabilitation, I learn how to use them. At first, they feel heavy, requiring so much energy I can't help but feel exhausted. Then, like breaking from chains, I feel my arms go free. The same process takes less time with my legs, and soon, I am on my feet. I look at my watch. All three hands point straight up toward the twelve. As I continue to stare down at my wrist, I notice the seconds hand start ticking and know right away that my watch isn't telling me what time it is. It is counting the time that I have been in the dream world. Whether it is dream seconds or real seconds, I don't know.

I absorb myself in my new achievement, forgetting for a moment why I am here in the first place. Not two seconds later, I hear a loud thud from inside the office, and I know exactly who is on the way. I race toward the door leading into the office, opening it with a hard pull, running into the maze of cubicles. It's a different maze than in the real world. I feel it form itself around my thoughts, creating turns and walls where I want them. I can't quite control these changes, however. Instead, it's almost like a protection formed by my subconscious. I need a place to hide, and the feeling of need creates this intricate maze that I alone know how to solve.

After running far enough into the maze, I stop to wait for the familiar signs that the hooded man is on his way. He usually wants me to hear him coming from far away, or at least I thought he did. After not hearing anything for some time, a loud crash booms from the meeting room I've just left. I know at once that it isn't him trying to scare me. He is angry. The door to the meeting room slams open, crashing against the wall so hard I can feel the vibrations across the room.

"Come out, come out, wherever you are," he says in a voice that sounds both playful and dangerous. As he moves through the room searching for me, he continues talking. "So, what's your endgame, little boy? Don't you realize yet that I am inevitable?"

I hear his footsteps as they move closer to where I'm hiding. As the man approaches, I do my best to stay quiet, trying hard not to think of anything in case he has a connection to my thoughts. After several minutes of waiting for the inevitable, I realize that the he can't find me. Then something clicks in my head — the man must be alerted to me entering the dream. He isn't the all-powerful, omniscient monster I thought he was. If I can get away from the area where I enter the dream, I will have plenty of time to figure out how to manipulate this world while I hide. I look down at my watch again. I've already been dreaming for five minutes, according to the movement of the long hand on my watch. How my watch is doing this, I do not know. But I trust it. The only issue is that Waldo is late in waking me, if my watch is correct.

Suddenly, I feel a tug on my shoulder, and my stomach drops to the floor. I am caught. I don't turn around or move the slightest bit. Instead I sit, paralyzed with fear. When nothing else happens for a few seconds, I turn to see what is behind me. Nothing. My only thought is that Waldo might be trying to wake me. I'm right. Another tug at my shoulder sends me crashing into the wall next to me. The sound from me crashing into the wall is loud enough I know it doesn't go unheard.

"There you are!" The man screams with a frenzy of joy, like a child finding another in hide and seek.

As his booming footsteps grow louder, the walls around me begin crashing down. Instead of focusing on this, I close my eyes and think as hard as I can about waking up. It doesn't work. I sit trapped in indecision, trying my hardest to escape my dreams as the weight of the man and room closes in around me. I remember my past dreams when I felt trapped, the fear that gripped me in those moments, and how I used to get out of them. A black cloth robe now stands in front of me, and as my eyes slowly crawl toward his torso, I decide I don't want to look into the man's eyes ever again and start shaking my head violently like a petulant child.

When I open my eyes again, Waldo's face is only inches from mine. He's standing over me, shaking my shoulders vigorously.

"I'm here, Waldo," I say, grabbing my head, now splitting in two from the pain. "I'm back."

Chapter XXIII

I sit up fast, holding my head to keep my brain from sloshing around. I've felt this way often after waking myself. It usually doesn't last long after I wake, but this time the bell in my head rings long after. It might be forty-five seconds in real time, but it feels like ten minutes. Something else happens this time as well. While the bell in my head continues to ring, I am unable to clearly remember if I'm still in the dream world or not. I pull my hands away from my face, and as my eyes vibrate in and out of focus, I see the world I just left and the one I'm trying to stay in switching back and forth like a flipbook.

"Are you okay, man?" I hear Waldo's voice, still not fully sure that I am back.

"Yeah, I'm okay," I say, as the ringing in my head and vibrating vision finally stops. I go through my routine of looking at my watch just to be sure. A sense of pride flushes over me as I realize that I'm back and my plan worked.

"I was able to move," I say confidently. "I've never been able to do that before."

"That's awesome, man!" I can tell he truly is excited, but Waldo will never truly understand this success. I'm still happy he is here to help me.

"There's one more thing," I say, turning serious. "If I move within the first moments of the dream and go somewhere else, he isn't able to find me as fast. I don't think he's able to sense where I am. I think he may be told when I enter the dream somehow and then he just goes to the place that I come in."

"I wonder if it matters where you enter," Waldo says. "Since you went to sleep here, did it take him longer to find you?"

"I'm not sure," I say, "but it is a good question to ask. It did seem to take longer for him to reach me, but only because I was focused on learning to move."

We decided to put Waldo's hypothesis to the test the next time I enter the dream world.

Chapter XXIV

We talk for the next hour, deciding that tomorrow might be a good day to try again. Next time, we would go to his place and see if switching locations helps to throw the man off. My body and mind wane from exhaustion, but a large weight feels lifted from my brain. Because of this, I decide it will be okay to stay up one more night. I make the short walk home where I shower and change into sweatpants and a sweatshirt before heading back to campus. Tonight, I will spend my all-nighter working on my paper for my Literature Analyses class.

I arrive at the library a little after nine p.m., making a quick stop at the Starbucks downstairs before finding an open work room tucked away toward the back of the fourth floor. The library is open twenty-four hours a day, so I am able to stay until my next class or until I am finished, whichever comes first.

The first few hours, I don't get much writing done. I have a hard-enough time wrapping my head around the book *As I Lay Dying* itself, let alone the analyses of another author. When I finally get a limited understanding of the two, the words flow freely onto the page. It doesn't take long before I have a solid four-page rough draft. The assignment guidelines state that the paper is to be five to six pages in length. I know from experience that my professor will not grade an assignment if it doesn't fit her requirements exactly.

By seven a.m., I am exhausted. My brain feels swollen, possibly from too much coffee, a lack of water, a lack of sleep, or the cramming of five and a half pages of writing. It isn't clear to me whether those pages are good or not. I hardly understood what I was supposed to do with the assignment; I did my best to make it seem like I know what I am talking about though. THe final product is an excellent balance of B.S. that I've worked to perfect throughout my time in college. Just enough to get a B, I hope.

I walk home to take a shower and eat breakfast as the dark of the night begins to break and soften. The sun has still not peeked over the horizon, birds are not yet in the mood to chirp, and streetlights continue to light the empty streets. I take the walk slowly, not wanting to stop for too long. I am at the point in my exhaustion now where I fear I will fall asleep if my feet stop moving for even a second.

As I approach the typically busy road dividing campus from my street, the pain in my head comes back, and soon, so does the disorientation I felt before. I clutch my head and close my eyes, trying my best not to trip into the street. I'm unsure if I'm still on the sidewalk or not, but trust that my feet have not stepped off yet. I begin to feel as I did waking up, unsure if I am still in the real world or the dream world. I try to move my hands from the sides of my head so that I can look at my watch and perform my reality check, but the pain is too much. I sit down to keep from falling, pushing both hands against the sides of my head as hard as I can to keep it from splitting in two.

When the pain subsides, the disorientation eases also. Again, I am unaware of how much time went by during this episode of confusion and pain. I open my eyes again to see three girls standing on the other side of the street, waiting for traffic to thin before crossing the road toward me. I stand up, hoping they haven't seen too much of what I was doing, and we all cross at the same interval of traffic. The girls all make an obvious effort to avoid eye contact with me as we pass each other.

"They must think I am crazy," I say under my breath.

After arriving home, I take a long, hot shower, sitting in the bottom of the tub as the water pours down over my outstretched legs. The steady stream of water relaxes my muscles enough that I begin craving a nap more than anything. It becomes harder and harder to tell myself no, and just as my eyes quit fighting, the water turns cold, snapping me out of my trance.

"It might be a little more difficult to stay awake today." As I say this, I look in the mirror, noticing for the first time the dark, coin-purse bags under my eyes.

Chapter XXV

By nine a.m., it's nearly impossible to stay awake. As I sit in my living room watching television, my head nods involuntarily toward my chest with each long blink of my eyes. Every time my eyes close, I feel the comfort of a long sleep pulling me further and further into its dark abyss. My body feels relaxed, and for the first time in a while, I don't fear the dreams to come. All I see is darkness. I'm comfortable and don't question it.

Then, I hear the sound of a knock at the door. For a moment, these knocks are followed by sheer panic. 'I'm not ready for this,' I scream inside my head. Jumping to my feet, the pain from before shoots straight to my head while my mind strains to decide if I'm still in a nightmare or hearing the door knock for real. I move slowly toward the door, still in the process of trying to form some sort of thought. I look at my watch; the time is normal, not counting the minutes. This reassures me and the confusion lessens as I finally set my thoughts straight. The pain eases as I open the door slowly, allowing the light from outside to pour into the dimly lit room.

Waldo stands in front of me, his eyebrows furrowed in a concerned look. "Are you okay, Elliot?" he asks, his voice cracking slightly. If I couldn't tell already that he was concerned, I know it now. Waldo has always been a little more sensitive than normal people, but he has never shown up at my door without calling or texting — especially so early in the morning. I am thankful. "You look like hell," he says. I can tell he says this trying to make me laugh, but I don't have the mental power to respond to his sense of humor this morning.

"I feel miserable," I confess. "I just pulled an all-nighter again, and I think it's starting to get to me." Waldo walks inside and sits down in the small green armchair next to the living room window. I explain how it feels like a switch turned in my brain and how I now have to fight headaches that split my skull apart and disorientation so bad I can't decide if I am still dreaming or not.

"How long have you been without a good amount of sleep?" he asks. I can see the gears in Waldo's mind turning. I don't have enough time for a response before he continues. "I think we may need to have you sleep twice today so that you can actually get some rest, man. I'm not a pre-med student, but I know that a lack of sleep will start to mess with your mind."

"The guy did say that he would start messing with me if I chose to stay awake," I say, knowing that this is exactly the reason.

Waldo's eyebrows furrow toward his nose in deep concentration. "Do you really think he has that much power?" he asks. "Like, is he walking about in your subconscious with a pair of bolt cutters, clipping wires?"

This gets me thinking. I can picture the no-named man whistling as he walks from room to room in my subconscious breaking whatever he can along the way.

"I'm not quite sure," I say, thinking hard about it. "It feels like he is disconnected from me. Like there's another person in the dream with me that somehow has always been there. When I was in the dream the last time, he had no idea where I was, so he must not be able to read my thoughts."

"Should we try seeing if you can make that connection?" Waldo asks. "I wonder if you concentrated hard enough—"

I cut him off before he continues. "I don't think I want to try that just yet," I say, shivering at the thought of opening my mind to him.

Chapter XXVI

Opening my eyes, I immediately look down at the watch on my wrist to make sure I'm still sleeping. Waldo and I have decided it is best if I sleep for one hour before class and no more. This is meant to charge my batteries more than it is to practice. At one hour, without fail, I hear Waldo's voice from the depths of my sleep and then I feel the heavy tug of his hand on my shoulder. Before going to sleep, I made sure to recite the mantra, "I will be aware," so that if I did stay longer, I would be able to move around. I also made a conscious note of what Waldo's voice sounded like so that I could focus on it easier.

Emerging from sleep this time, I don't experience the agonizing headache or the disorientation that I would have from shaking myself awake. We determine that this will be how I sleep until I get better at lucid dreaming.

Now entering the third night without much sleep, it is way past messing with my mind. Just walking to class, I check my watch multiple times to remember that I am awake and not experiencing a dream or a weird kind of déjà vu. As I walk down the street toward campus, the combination of a failing mind and lack of sleep soon begin to create hallucinations — stop signs bend in the direction of their shadows as I approach, gusts of wind carrying leaves and dust appear more like wraiths floating along the ground toward their victims. I can't imagine experiencing this at night, I think to myself. What am I even doing out here?

I make it to class and take my usual seat in the back of the room. I'm not sure what class I am in. The name escapes me like a word on the tip of my tongue. It doesn't matter anyway. From the time I enter the class, I become fascinated with the faces around me. Everyone's eyes appear sunk deep in their head. Dark blue veins sprout from the center of what I now think of as pits; deep, dark pits where their eyes should be.

I don't make it long, about ten minutes, before getting out of my seat and quietly walking out of class. I know I'm not dreaming. My watch is still operating on 'real' time when I look. I walk to the office as fast as I can manage without running. On the way, I pass by more sunken faces and decide to keep my head down for the time I'm outside. When I get to the student media building, however, things are much worse.

As I meander my way through the cubicle maze to my desk, the first person I see is Stephanie, our editor-in-chief. She is sporting her usual stern mood and looks just a little more evil than usual with her eyes sunk deep into her head. She attempts to ask me what I have planned for the next edition of our paper, but I have much more on my plate to deal with, so I try to ignore her for the moment.

"I'm not feeling too well," I say, pushing past her toward my desk.

Hannah and Waldo are already at their desks, with their headphones in. We took to this strategy early in the year to avoid talking to Stephanie. She tends to pick her favorites and anyone else not a part of her trio of friends catches her mostly at her nasty times. It is best to just avoid her in general unless you have a question and a craving for a bad day.

Despite the lights in the office all being on, the room looks dreary and depressing, not helped by the many sunken faces occupying it.

I sit at my desk, pulling out my laptop like usual, and hear the rolling of wheels from Waldo's chair behind me.

"How are you feeling, man?" he asks from just behind my left shoulder. I turn to face him as I answer.

"Worse," I say, noticing that he also has sunken eyes and deep blue veins emerging from their depths. "Since you left this morning, my mind has started to go downhill." I point toward the door without saying anything; the secret sign that we should go get 'coffee'. We walk outside without another word, crossing the street toward the Student Union building where most of the coffee shops are located. "I think I'm beginning to hallucinate. This morning stop signs would bend as I passed, and now, everyone I see looks like they've joined some sort of demon army — their eyes are sunk deep in their heads and dark blue veins sprout from their centers. Even yours are like that."

Waldo turns away from me as we walk, facing forward more noticeably. "I've been thinking about it since last night," he says, sounding concerned. "Now that you're starting to hallucinate, it reinforces my idea even more."

I know deep down what Waldo is getting to, but being the one who has to do it, I don't want to hear.

"You have to stop hiding from him," Waldo says, staring me straight in the eyes for the first time in a few minutes. These words cut through me like a knife. I have been afraid for a long time, and I hoped to skip straight from fearful to courageous without noticing. "We have to beat him." Waldo's eyes are stern and serious. This confidence I have never seen from him. It gives me more confidence also. But Waldo won't be there with me when I go back to the dream world. I will have to find the confidence and courage to face my demon alone.

Chapter XXVII

Lying on my back on Waldo's couch, I keep my eyes staring straight toward the ceiling as I prepare to enter deep sleep. I do this mostly to remain focused, but also to avoid the sight of clutter that usually comes with the bachelor lifestyle. Waldo's apartment is less than endurable when it comes to cleanliness. I pick a clean spot on the ceiling and keep my eyes there without budging.

"Are you almost ready?" he asks with a hint of nervousness in his voice.

I plan to sleep for two and a half hours, which will stick me in the dream world for an hour. At the end of this time, Waldo will wake me the usual way. If I get into trouble before that, it is up to me to get myself out. My goal is to find a way to beat the hooded man. For now, I don't have a clue as to how I will do it or if it is even possible. All I want is a peaceful night's sleep without someone watching over me. I know I won't get it by simply asking for it, so I have to find some way to take it.

I'm not ready, but I nod my head yes before reciting my mantra, "I will be aware when I dream. I will be aware when I dream."

The last thing I hear as I drift off to sleep is the quiet whisper of Waldo's voice. "Good luck, buddy."

Chapter XXVIII

I open my eyes, and I am still staring at the spot on the ceiling. At first, I feel like I'm still awake, but a quick glance at my watch informs me that I have successfully entered the dream. It takes me no time at all to gain movement in my arms and legs and soon I am walking toward Waldo's front door. I need to get out of his apartment to avoid being caught. I reach the front door and as my hand touches the door knob, I wait for just a moment, listening. Usually, he would be here by now, or at the very least, I would feel his presence. This time, however, there is no loud knock or a feeling that everything is closing in. There is hooded figure. The only thought that crosses my mind is that switching beds must have worked to confuse him.

Continuing to clutch the cold door knob, I turn the handle slowly, allowing the weight of the door to open itself after it clicks open. Peering outside through a crack in the door, I see only a desolate street, deprived of anyone else. There are cars of course, and everything I'd typically see in this neighborhood, but no one walking the streets like normal. I open the door wider, stepping through the entryway into the outside world. A quiet blanket covers the air outside Waldo's apartment.

I pull the door toward me, making sure I hear an audible click to make sure it is secure. There are no numbers on this door and many others look like it, so I decide to crack it back open just a little. I'd rather let the cat in than lose my way.

When I turn from the door, I'm startled to see a man standing in front of me wearing tattered gray robes. He isn't staring at me but looking in the direction of the stairs that lead down the landing to the sidewalk. I stand, rooted in the same spot, contemplating my next move.

"I am not here to hurt you, Elliot," he says in a voice that reminds me of Waldo's. I walk a few steps until I'm standing in front of this new person and am not surprised at all to see my friend.

"Waldo?" I ask. "What are you doing here?"

"I am not actually your friend, Waldo," the man says. "I am your dream guide, and this face is simply the one you've chosen to lead you."

At this, a thousand questions start rolling around in my head, but the right one eludes me for some time until the guide answers without me asking.

"I am a part of your subconscious," he says. "I know what you need far before you ask."

This comforts me some, but looking at his robes and their tattered state, I'm not sure if I should be comforted at all.

"Excuse my appearance," he says, waving the back of his hand at the thought to shoo it away. "I've been at war for a long time now, and it hasn't been going well as of late."

This sparks another ring of questions swirling through my thoughts, but he clears those up as well.

"The man you fear so much is not a man at all but a demon," the guide said. "He wants one thing — to take your body and trap your soul. I've been fighting him since you were twelve, and in the dream world, he has no equal. I've managed to keep him from the archives that hold your most important memories, however. If he reaches these, he can break your subconscious and give you his own memories. I don't know what might happen after that, but you wouldn't be you." The guide sighs at this. His head bows to the point that his chin touches his chest.

"I'm here to stop him," I say, with an air of confidence that I know is false. "Have you figured out how we might do that?"

The dream guide shakes his head. "Not at all," he says. "The few times I've gotten close to him, he overpowered me, and I barely escaped. I do know that he never leaves that pink house you live in. Not unless he senses that you've come into the dream through another entry point."

This is where we will start. We begin walking in the direction of my house. Waldo's apartment is only a ten-minute walk from my tiny pink house. I look at my watch and see that five minutes have passed since entering this dream. Plenty of time to at least nose around.

"Where were you all the other times?" I turn to the guide as we walk down the street. "Why were you never here before?"

"You've never made it this far," the guide says. "I've been waiting for you to get out of bed."

Chapter XXIX

We walk for nearly a half mile without speaking a word. When we reach an empty parking lot on the corner of an empty intersection, we stop.

Dream Waldo turns to me before speaking. "We have to run through a few things before I let you walk into that house," he says, pointing to the empty parking lot. "I would like you to imagine a car in that spot there — whatever car you want."

I'm not sure where this is going, but maybe a car would get us there faster. I concentrate on the spot he pointed, trying to imagine a car there.

Nothing happens.

"Well, this is kind of difficult," I say, giving a small chuckle.

"I would love to hear you say that in about ten minutes," the guide says. "Do you think it will be any more or less funny then?"

I see his point and try harder. This time, I use the trick I learned for lucid dreaming — pushing my finger through the palm of my hand. Instead of just seeing it in the spot, I feel it sitting there. When I stop concentrating, the car is still in the spot I'd imagined.

"Not bad at all," he says. "Now block this." Without me turning to look, the man throws a rock in my direction. As I turn to see it, I simultaneously put an arm up to defend the side of my face. The rock stops before hitting me, skipping off the space in front of my arm and landing a few feet away. I continue looking at the spot where the rock should have hit me. In the space in front of my arm, a small, nearly invisible shield has formed.

"Your mind is a lot stronger than you think, Elliot," the guide says. "As soon as you need a tool, weapon, protection or anything else you can imagine, it will materialize. There will be no lag, as you say, unless you are indecisive with what you need. In these situations, your mind will act to protect your body. It will happen again, but these protections are not strong enough to withstand the demon for too long." With this, he holds his hand out in front of me as if he wants to give me something. In his hand materializes a blanket. Not just any blanket — the one I use on my bed.

I laugh again.

"You can take this as seriously as you like," he says with extreme patience. "But have no doubt, this is a matter of you living or… something much worse than death."

I take the blanket from him. "What do I use this for?" I ask seriously.

"Do you remember all those times you lay in bed, knowing the demon was right there with you somehow?"

I do remember these times.

"As near as I can guess, he was never able to get you because this," (he held up one side of the blanket) "somehow kept him from touching you." He stares straight at me, judging my reaction. I remember a few times I was aware that the hooded man was with me. My foot would be outside the covers, and I would get this growing feeling that pulling it inside was the best thing to do at that very moment. "Now, imagine that seconds before you pulled your foot back under the covers," he says, demonstrating the movement, "he was hovering over you, itching to grab that ankle and pull you out of bed."

I shiver as goose bumps sweep across my body. He needn't say any more. I pull the blanket over my back and tie it around my neck like a cape. It's a little long, dragging on the ground, so I imagine it's the size of an actual cape and as soon as I think about its shape, the blanket shortens itself.

"Your cape should be the only thing he can't get through," the guide says. "You'll need more than that, however."

Chapter XXX

We walk down the street until we cross a large, four-lane bridge I'm familiar with. "Only about five minutes left before we reach the house," I say, my voice waning as I finish the sentence.

"Do you have a plan?" the guide asks. The dream version of Waldo was so similar to the real one.

"Even in the dream world, you ask questions you already know the answer to." I laugh. "Of course I don't."

As we near the house, my mind begins to fish for anything that I might be able to do in this place. To my understanding, I will be able to do anything I want here if I can just imagine it. This turns out to be easier than I thought.

With every block, I practice my new-found skill, and to Dream Waldo's surprise, I pick it up quickly. I can move objects that are already in the dream, change them, and make them bend to my will. I practice creating mazes, like the one in my work office. Many times throughout the journey, I have to go back to help Waldo through. I'm not sure if he is really lost or just trying to build my confidence. Either way, it works.

At one point, I'm having so much fun testing my own creativity, I hardly realize we are a block from the house. We should have been able to see the house for the past two hundred yards, but something tells me my guide wanted me to keep my mind off it until we got here, like a parent guarding their child from the realities of adulthood.

"Are you coming?" Dream Waldo asks from a few feet ahead.

Without realizing it, I have stopped dead in my tracks seeing the tiny, pink house vibrantly standing out against a dull gray background. It is a beacon, I think — a message to whomever enters this world.

"Here I am," it says.

Chapter XXXI

"Any last words of advice?" I ask, taking a deep breath as I stand at the intersection between the sidewalk and path leading to the front door. I begin to feel a presence inside the house, and I feel as though I'm being pulled closer.

"Good luck, my friend," I hear Waldo say from behind me.

For the next twenty steps leading to the door, I hardly notice my feet touch the ground. It's like my body is on autopilot, disconnected from my thoughts. My hand is on the door knob before I make the mental connection to what I'm doing. "Stop!" A voice calls from the back of my subconscious. I take a deep breath, using the small moment to process my next step. It's now or never, I think to myself, gathering up the last bit of courage I can. With another deep breath, I put my hand on the door knob and turn it.

When the door opens, I stand in the entryway for what seems like a lifetime, waiting for something strange to happen or for someone to jump out at me. The living room of the pink house looks exactly like the one from my world, including the small green armchair and three-person sofa. I will have to walk two more steps inside before I'll be able to see the hallway to my bedroom and the one to the kitchen. Just one step feels like a mile, however. I lift my left foot off the ground, placing it as gently as I can on the thick, shag carpet. I repeat the same motion with my right foot, placing it more gently than my left. Before I can think about another step, the door forces itself closed behind me so hard and fast that it sends a gust of wind through the house and a row of goosebumps up my spine.

"I can smell your fear from here," a voice says calmly from one of the rooms of the house. I think for a second that it might have come from the kitchen, but this is a dream and the house seems much larger inside than I remember it being. "I'm disappointed that you tried to fight your fate, but you're here now to accept your punishment, so I guess I forgive you." His laughter cuts like a knife as it echoes throughout the house.

"I'm not here to accept punishment," I say, feeling anger boil inside me. These were the first words I'd ever spoken to him, and I could tell he was a little surprised that I spoke at all.

"You've come a long way from that small child who used to let me torment his siblings rather than face me," he says coldly, reminding me of years before when I hardly had the courage to tighten my blanket from the fear that he would know I wasn't sleeping.

"My understanding of your tactics was lacking in those years," I say sternly.

"Ah, but time has not changed much, little boy." I can hear his voice growing closer in the shadows of the kitchen. "Just the other day, you were still too terrified to face me. The fact that you are here is nothing more than necessity and more fear pushing you toward an inevitable fate."

"So, what is it that you want?" I ask, stepping slowly toward the hallway on my right leading to my bedroom. I am stalling at this point. I scan the house while the voice speaks from the kitchen, formulating the first steps of what I think is a plan.

"All will be revealed shortly," the voice says, his footsteps now audibly walking across the linoleum kitchen floor.

At the sound of this, I run down the hallway toward my room. The hallway connecting the living room to my bedroom is only three feet, but I imagine it to be longer as I work up to a full sprint. I run straight for maybe twenty feet and then turn right where the hallway immediately extends to more than forty feet. As I continue running down this path, I look right and left as many times as I can, creating new paths that meander endlessly throughout the dream. I run for what seems like five minutes, creating paths that span for days and walls covered in mirrors so that once the man finds himself inside, I can trap him.

That is my plan, anyway.

"Another maze, I see." The voice echoes throughout the halls mockingly. Soon, black smoke begins to seep through the shag carpet floor. At first, I think it might be fire, but that thought quickly vanishes when my feet feel a painful sensation like thousands of needles sticking up from the floor. I look at my feet and see my shoes are being eaten away by this 'acid' smoke. The smoke continues to fill the floor of the maze, beginning its ever quickening pace up the walls.

I search my memory for anything that might help me out of this situation. The burning sensation around my legs is now at my thighs. I need to climb, I think out loud, and in the same breath, a solution appears. In front of me stands a tall ladder, which looks like it will reach the top of my tall maze wall. When I reach the top, the house is gone. Miles around me, all I see is the maze I've created and smoke wafting from the tops of the walls like a poorly built chimney. I imagine the entire space closed off and smooth again like an endless parking lot, and as quickly as the idea passes through my mind, it happens. I create a parking lot even Disneyland can't fill.

Far in the distance, I see the mirage of the hooded figure walking toward me. I blink once, and when my eyelids flip open again, he is standing only a few feet from me. Without another wasted word, the man lunges, reaching his milky-white hand toward my throat. I react as quickly as possible, spinning to my right, throwing the blanket over my body. I'm only hoping for a few seconds of protection while I come up with my next move. It works. As I sit inside my blanket plotting, I can hear the man on the outside raging against the soft shell surrounding me. I peek under a small crack I create between the ground and the blanket, but as I put the right side of my face to the ground and look out with only one eye, I see him staring straight back.

"Hello, little boy," the man says, clearly playing with his meal before enjoying the taste of adrenaline that now runs through my veins. I see this as a moment I should take advantage of. Simultaneously flipping the blanket off with my left hand, I swing with my right toward his jaw, focusing on all the pain and fear he has caused me over the years and channeling it into the end of my fist. I feel my knuckles connect on the thin bone structure of the man's face and watch as he staggers backwards a few steps. He doesn't wipe his lip to check for blood or even wince at the pain like the bad guys I'd seen in movies, but he is surprised. So am I.

I look from my balled up right hand to him, and back to my fist. I realize at this moment that I have only succeeded in pissing him off. With every bit of energy remaining, I focus on being somewhere else, anywhere else. Nothing happens. I concentrate on a specific place, the pink house. Without trying much harder than that, I find myself standing in my living room again. I'm alone for now, but I can feel the man coming toward the house and know I have only seconds. I look down at my watch out of habit and see that I only have a minute before Waldo will try to wake me.

As the thought of safety vanishes from my thoughts, it is quickly replaced by the sound of the front door knob turning and the click of the lock opening. Rather than run and hide, I turn to face the door that now stands ajar. The unnamed man, now standing where I had first entered, smiles in a way that I have seen only once before. It's a smile that says, 'We both know this is the end'.

I'm not thinking this at all, however. I have one more play in this short game of chess. I remember what Waldo suggested before I entered the dream — try connecting to his thoughts. When he first brought it up, the idea scared me. If I had access to his brain, it would allow him access to mine. I wouldn't be able to keep the connection for long. Just a second. I only needed a long enough time to imagine something like a computer virus and plant it deep in his mind so that it would destroy him from the inside.

Without thinking much more, I close my eyes as tight as I can make them, pressing my eyelids together until they hurt from concentrating. I focus on the man's presence in the room, and as I continue to think of him, I feel the churning of gears in his head trying to guess what I might do next. He is waiting for me at this point, unafraid of anything I can offer in the way of defense. I lock on to this feeling, imagining a cord running from my head to his.

"I know what you're trying to do, and it won't work here." His voice cuts through the back of my mind, momentarily freezing my concentration and the cord now slithering toward his ear. "You can't escape this dream. This house prevents you from doing that now."

"That's not at all what I'm doing," I say, gritting my teeth in concentration.

The slow crawling cord reaches the side of the man's ear, connecting firmly inside. At this, he winces, attempting to clear his ear out with a finger. The invisible cord is still attached, and as I refocus on the virus to plant it in his subconscious, a cold liquid feeling starts to trickle into my ear. He is trying to get into my mind. The thought processes too late for me to act. I've already kept the connection too long, and now, he is in control again. I try pulling the cord from my own mind, but the man across from me just shakes his head, laughing.

"Not quite the method I thought you would use, but I figured you'd be fishing around in my thoughts sooner or later," the man says, smiling wider than before. "You asked me what I wanted a few minutes ago."

As he walks slowly toward me, I try to move away, to do anything. Nothing. I'm as stuck as I was at fourteen years old, lying in my bed in a dusty trailer, staring at the cloaked figure that would rule my thoughts for the next ten years. The man reaches out for my throat again. This time, I feel his cold hand wrap around my airway, his thumb and index finger connecting at the back of my neck.

“You’ve given me what I wanted all along,” he says, wrapping his finger in the cord connecting us like he is talking on an old landline phone. The liquid continues to trickle in through my ear and down my throat until I’m unable to speak. Soon, the room around me begins to fade until there’s only darkness. He’s choking the life from me, I think, as the edges of my vision close in. With my final thoughts, I cling to life, reaching as hard as I can for the surface above me, too far out of reach.

Chapter XXXII

When the darkness fades away, I'm lying on a couch again, staring at a white spot on the ceiling. For a moment, I feel a rush of excitement. "Did I beat him?" I wonder aloud.

"No, you didn't." I recognize the voice immediately as the dream version of Waldo.

Sitting up abruptly, my excitement fades just as fast, replaced quickly by anger and embarrassment that I couldn't have put up a better match.

"If it makes you feel any better to know," Dream Waldo said, flipping through the channels on the television. "You didn't really have a chance in the first place."

"I would have, if you were here," I say, glaring at my subconscious.

"I am not meant to fight this beast," he says, turning from the television, returning my glare sternly. "My sole purpose is to protect your memories and the door to your subconscious. If I were to fall, your battle would be over."

"Where is he now?" I ask, standing as if to go somewhere.

"You'll see," he says, nodding his head to the TV screen.

For the next few moments, we sit in silence as he continues flipping through channels. There are no numbers, and after every ten channels, they seem to start over. Minutes pass by. I begin to say something, but I'm cut off before I open my mouth to speak.

"This looks like it might be good," he says, placing the remote on the small, square coffee table in front of him that wasn't in my house before that very moment.

I look toward the forty-two-inch TV across the room and all that I see is a blurry, unfocused white spot. From the look of it, the camera seems to be staring at the ceiling. And then it clicks — we are looking through my eyes in the 'real' world.

Chapter XXXIII

I turn to face the TV, focusing on the white spot on the ceiling. Soon after adjusting in my seat, something pops into the focus of the TV screen. Waldo's face now peers down at us as if we are stuck at the bottom of a deep well.

"Elliot, Elliot!" Waldo pleads from above.

And then, it happens. The 'camera' pans left and then right before settling back on Waldo's face. The demon is in my body.

"What happened?" Waldo's voice sounds concerned. "I had a hard time waking you up, man. I thought you were stuck for a second."

The man, now inhabiting my body, sits up so that we have a straight view of Waldo sitting on the coffee table next to his couch.

Cupping his face in both hands, he smiles his wide-mouthed smile, much different from my own. "We beat him," he says.

"Really?" Waldo asks, jumping to his feet. "That's so awesome, man!" He pulls the imposter Elliot up by the armpits, hugging him so that our only view is of an ear, hair and the wall of the nasty apartment.

Waldo holds us in this position for nearly thirty seconds before stepping away and looking us up and down. "Are you okay, man?" Waldo asks, the concern in his voice coming back. "I thought you'd be more excited about this. I mean, he's been haunting you all your life, hasn't he?"

The imposter Elliot pauses briefly before coming to an answer. "You're right, he has." Imposter Elliot's voice sounds almost prideful at this. "I'm just tired and ready for a new life."

Waldo seems satisfied with this answer, and I find myself yelling at the TV like a crazed fan hoping their favorite character sees through the tricks of the bad guy. "That's not me, Waldo!" I plead with the screen. "You have to realize this!"

"From what we see, he doesn't," Dream Waldo says.

We continue to watch Waldo through the TV as he and the imposter Elliot talk about the events of the dream.

"He was really strong," imposter Elliot lies. "I wasn't sure how I would stop him, but eventually I tired him out and trapped him in the pink house."

"How did you tire him out?" Waldo asks, with one eyebrow raised skeptically. "And how did you trap him? It seemed like he was much more powerful than that."

"I created a maze, and when he ran inside it to get me, I locked the door behind him," the imposter says, growing more confident with his answers as he tells them. "I guess the lock I created was stronger than I thought it would be."

"Hmmm, that was easy then," Waldo says, washing away all skepticism from his expression and managing a smile. "I'm happy for you, man."

"Thanks… man," the imposter responds awkwardly. "Satisfied?"

This is surely the slip of the tongue Waldo needs if nothing else is to clue him in on this obvious imposter.

Waldo glances in our direction quickly with one eye, then mumbles under his breath, "Huh? Oh, yeah. Totally, man."

Chapter XXXIV

"Waldo must know the imposter is in my skin," I think out loud as I pace around the living room. This feeling only grows stronger as we see Waldo asking the new Elliot if he'd like to hang out tonight.

"That's good," I say to the television. "Keep him there."

The imposter declines, saying he has a lot of work to do that night.

"Homework on a Friday?" Waldo asks quizzically, moving to the kitchen without turning his back. "I've never known you to do homework on the weekend."

I can tell that Waldo is on to him at this point, but I hope deep down the new Elliot doesn't realize this.

"Are you hungry?" Waldo asks. "We can get some food."

After he declines again, Waldo walks out of the screen, returning after the microwave sounds in the background. Waldo walks back into our view holding a plate of chicken stacked two pieces high. I also see the handle of a steak knife on the edge of the plate. Before I think to question the use of a steak knife on chicken, I realize that Waldo is protecting himself.

"He's figured it out," I say, smiling as I do.

As he begins to eat, Waldo holds out a drumstick, offering it to the new Elliot. "Are you sure, man? It's good," he says through a mouthful of chicken when the offer is declined. To make things more awkward, Waldo keeps the TV off so that the room is silent except for the sounds of flesh separating from bone and the sloppy chewing that follows. All we hear or see for ten minutes is a greasy-faced Waldo eating chicken bones down to their core. He knows this man is not me, and he is trying to bide as much time as possible for me to figure something out.

The imposter Elliot continues watching Waldo eat like a pig, unsure of the proper rules and customs of watching someone eat. I've known Waldo long enough to know that this meal might not end for a while, depending on how hungry he was at the start. The longer he watches, however, the more the imposter becomes impatient. We can feel it as his frustration grows.

"Are you almost done with your meal?" he asks more than once. "I would like to go home so I can get ready."

"Ready for what?" The greasy-faced Waldo asks, mouth still stuffed with chicken. "I thought we were going to hang out for a bit?"

"I said no," the man says, growing angry.

"Okay, you can stop now, Waldo," I say to the screen, hoping he will listen. "I think he's getting angry."

The warning doesn't make it. Without another bite, the man stands from his chair and moves to within inches of Waldo, towering over him.

"You know, don't you?" The imposter moves fast enough that Waldo doesn't realize what's going on, which is probably for the best. The steak knife, placed precisely between two vertebrae, kills Waldo before his bottom jaw closes on the mouthful of food he is chewing.

"Noooo!" I scream toward the T.V., dropping to my knees in front of it. My hands clasp pleading for the moment to come back. "No. No. No. No." My hands grasp at the hairs on my head as I attempt to comprehend what just happened to my friend.

Chapter XXXV

As we watch through the small, dream-world TV, the imposter Elliot continues to stand in place for more than a minute, letting the stream of blood from Waldo's neck slow to a trickle and then a methodical drip. The man's breathing is heavy with adrenaline still coursing through his veins.

"Did you think it would end any differently?" the voice asks us, now moving through the room to the hallway bathroom. He looks in the mirror, so we can see his/my face as he talks. "I always planned to kill your friend. I figured you could see his last meal. Although, I'm not sure if you should have seen him like that in his last moments now that I think about it. I mean, eating like a pig covered in grease." The man laughs at this, turning on the faucet to wash his hands in the sink.

"You didn't tell anyone else about me, did you?" he asks, staring straight into my eyes in the mirror. After a long pause, he turns off the water and stands tall in the mirror, admiring his new body. "I guess I'll have to go see for myself."

Chapter XXXVI

Dream Waldo clicks the remote, turning off the TV. As I watch the image disappear, I lunge, reaching for the man in the image with no success. He is gone. I spin, turning my anger toward the only person in the room.

"Why did you turn that off?" I demand an answer. "What if he goes after one of my other friends?"

"He will," Waldo says. "And what he does to them, you can't control from here. What you can control is what happens when he gets back here. If you fail again, then more will die."

The weight of this thought sits heavily on my chest. I can't accept that the few friends I have left will soon be gone. I keep hoping that somehow this is all a dream, but I know it isn't. The reality of it is too much to bear, so I try not to dwell on it. I have to prevent more people from dying while I watch helplessly from the sidelines.

"Nothing I do affects him," I say, after a long silence. "I don't think I can kill him."

"And he knows that," Dream Waldo says, with a touch of sarcasm.

"You don't have to be an asshole," I say, raising my voice. "I just watched my friend die by the hands of someone I've been afraid of my whole life, and you want to make light of it." I walk to the door in two quick steps and have my hand on the knob when Waldo continues.

"Don't you see how that works to your advantage?" he asks. "He doesn't fear you at all. Which means he probably won't wait three days to sleep like you did, and he won't hide from you either. He'll come for you."

Dream Waldo is right. He wasn't afraid of me and would most likely beat me again if I fought him straight up. The one advantage I did see is that he would search me out. This meant that I got to choose the battlefield.

Immediately, I'm reminded of what the unnamed man told me before I connected to his mind. "This house prevents you from leaving the dream world now."

"He must have put some sort of curse on it," I think out loud. I'm not sure if the curse will work against him, but it seems like the best option to use as a trap. Because if he isn't afraid of me, I have no doubt that he will follow me in.

The only problem I have now is that a connection exists between the imposter and myself. For all I know, it is only enough to allow him to inhabit my body. Only, I think. As if this is something small. If he has this much power from the connection, there are bound to be other weaknesses he can exploit if the connection remains unbroken. With this, I realize I have another weapon.

I sit down on the couch, closing my eyes and concentrating on the connection between myself and the other Elliot. I visualize the cord connecting us, following it until I can see through his eyes into the real world. My heart leaps with hope when I see that he is only a block or so away from Waldo's house, and from what I can tell, he is lost. He continues walking until he approaches an intersection that I recognize — Main and Parkcenter. The imposter is far from campus and the student media building where most of the people I know are probably sitting, working on articles for the next issue of the paper. Upon recognizing that he is on the right path, imposter Elliot begins to walk faster.

I'm just a passenger in my own body, but passengers can grab the wheel if they want to crash the car, so I try. I focus on my right leg, using every ounce of energy I can to stop it from moving. It works. The other Elliot doesn't notice in time, tripping over what he thinks is a crack in the sidewalk and smacking his face on the cement. I flush with triumph, and the sight of blood dripping to the sidewalk as the man gets up tells me that he is feeling the pain. I continue holding the one leg still, while the imposter drags it behind him like a stump. Then, I focus on the other leg. This time, he catches himself with his hands just in time.

"You think you're clever, little boy?" he asks, spitting up blood again. "But any damage you do to this body, you will feel later. Or any damage that I do." His voice sounds cold, and I know he is willing to destroy my body if it comes to it. "Now, be a good little boy and give me back my legs, so I can go visit your friends."

Reluctantly, I release his legs and disconnect myself from his thoughts. If I can access his mind and control my body, then he will surely be able to do so when he is in this world. I will need to break this connection before I can go back to my own body.

It will take at least thirty minutes for the other Elliot to reach campus and then the student media building. Looking at my watch, I realize that I have been in this world for nearly four hours — the longest I'd been asleep in weeks. I set my timer for a half hour and begin thinking of a plan.

Chapter XXXVII

The imposter reaches the student media building a little later than I expect, but I'm not complaining about the extra time for my friends. I'm hoping that most people are gone by now. I'm not sure of the time, but it must be late considering the street lights are on, and to my amazement, the office lights aren't. My excitement is quickly replaced by the feeling of sickness as Elliot places his hand on the office door, and it opens. He walks through the darkness of the office, slowly toward the soft glow of a laptop screen illuminating the middle of the maze of cubicles.

As he approaches, the imposter stays on the other side of a cubicle wall, only inches from his unknown victim, his eyes barely able to see over the top.

He watches and makes me watch for the next five minutes as Hannah types away on her computer, oblivious to the world outside her own. She has her headphones in and isn't aware that anyone has entered the office.

"This one is almost too easy," The imposter says, walking slowly around the cubicle wall until he is only a foot behind her. Methodically, he turns toward the desk next to Hannah's, searching the drawers without her hearing a thing. When he finds a pair of scissors, the man takes a good moment to admire them. The black-handled scissors aren't of any special design; he just wants me to see the murder weapon before the final blow.

The imposter turns to face Hannah once more, performing a cutting motion in the air with the scissors like he is about to cut a piece of paper. As he closes the distance behind Hannah to less than six inches, I think for sure that she will feel his presence or at least smell his sweat from the long walk.

Unfortunately, Hannah isn't the most aware person at the best of times. She continues listening to music as the other Elliot raises his clasped hands, holding the scissors above her head. He's arrogant, and rather than swiftly taking his victim, he pauses to let me see how he will be doing the killing.

This split second is all I need. I take control of both arms, driving the pair of black-handled scissors deep into his right thigh. An inhuman scream pierces the office air, startling Hannah to her feet. Without even a glance behind her, she sprints through the maze of cubicles and out the front door into the night. The now crippled imposter stumbles after her, tripping over his own feet. He is new to the pains of being human and it shows as he cries out with every step.

Sitting on the carpet with his back against a cubicle wall, the other Elliot watches as the blood drains from his leg like a tipped over milk jug. As he slips from consciousness, he repeats the mantra mockingly, "I will be aware when I dream," laughing as he does so. "See you soon, little buddy."

Chapter XXXVIII

I stand outside the small, pink house making final changes before my visitor arrives. I create another maze, one that only becomes visible once entered, and place it in front of the small house. I then seal up the back door and all windows, molding them into continuous walls. The side with the front door, I leave looking as it normally does.

As the sky fills with dark storm clouds, the wind also starts to pick up until each gust nearly sweeps me off my feet. Then, far off on the horizon, a bolt of lightning splits the sky, creating a sound like an explosion as it hits the ground.

"He's here," I say, taking a deep breath.

I sit down on the curb in front of the pink house, waiting for him to show up. The wind continues to gust hard sideways, kicking up dust. This brings visibility to no more than a few feet in front of my face. Another bolt of lightning cuts though the horizon, revealing the outline of a hooded figure about twenty feet away. The image is there for only a second before it is dark again, but the outline of the man is burned into my retinas. In the next flash of lightning, the silhouette moves closer until it stands only ten feet away. The hooded figure's red eyes are all that remain in the empty dark of night.

I'm standing now, preparing myself for his first move. In the next flash of lightning, the hooded figure's image appears just inches in front of me. His hand grabs hold of my throat, the weight of his fingers crushing my airway. Concentrating through the pain, I follow the imaginary cord from my thoughts to his, trying my best to take control of his grip. It works. As he lets go of my neck, I turn and run toward the entrance of my invisible maze. I make it inside, running through the twists and turns I hope will hold the man up for at least a second. I can hear as he enters, smacking himself into one of the walls before discovering that I've put another maze in his way.

"Another maze?" he asks, laughing at the thought. "Haven't you learned?"

I have, I think as I sprint to the end of the short maze and through the front door of the pink house.

The maze proves to be nothing more than a speed bump as the unnamed man rips through its walls with a wave of his hand. On the other side of the door, I can hear the knob turning slowly as if the man on the other side is being cautious. The door creaks open just enough for him to slip inside.

The room is as dark as night. The only light comes from the single window at the front of the house, which allows only the tiniest bit of light in from each flash of the lightning outside. It's just enough to see the outline of larger objects in the room. The hooded figure moves slowly around the room looking for me. I tucked myself behind the TV stand before he entered, hoping he would move to other parts of the house before coming my way. "Come out, come out, wherever you are," he says playfully.

The hooded figure turns his back towards me, moving into the kitchen. As he does, he also, unknowingly, walks into another maze. The first maze was for show. This one was not. I quickly imagine the wall closed off to the kitchen, trapping him inside a funhouse I visited when I was a kid.

I remember how terrified it made me feel of my own image, trying to walk through a maze of mirrors that transformed my body into different shapes. Then, as you turn into what you think is a corner, it's just another mirror to smack you in the nose. You could always tell when someone was put through the ringer in one of these fun-houses; they would emerge with their hands outstretched in front of them, their steps short like an old lady with a walker.

To make things harder for the him, I tried my best to make the mirrors unbreakable. It was one thing to imagine them being so, but not everything was certain here. When I hear the first crash of a mirror being destroyed, I know it hasn't worked like I hoped.

I move from behind the TV toward the door. As I turn the handle, I imagine another fun-house in the living room, just to slow him down some more. I turn the handle. The door slams open with a gust of wind. The same gust continues to push the door open, preventing me from shutting it. As hard as I fight to shut it, the door feels as though someone is holding the other side just as hard. I grab the handle again, pulling with everything I have in me until it shuts with a loud bang, throwing me to the hard cement outside. Getting to my feet, I face the door again, this time imagining that the wall is like the other walls of the house — solid and continuous without a window or crack for a door.

"He's stuck," I say, remembering that he had said no one can wake up from the dream world once they enter the pink house. At that moment, a thundering crash hits the wall of the house on the other side of where the door used to be. Then another.

I remember the cord connecting myself to him, so I concentrate hard trying to break the connection. As my thoughts begin to focus on our connection, I feel him fighting through; the slow, cold liquid moving down the line and toward my own ear. The liquid gets closer and closer, but nothing I do works to sever the connection. I concentrate with all my will, trying to push the liquid back, but it keeps coming. Finally, I focus on my end of the cord, grabbing it with both hands and ripping it apart. With this, the cord splits, leaving the end attached to the unnamed man dangling in the wind like a single strand of a spider's web. A small piece remains attached to my own ear, but I'm confident that he hasn't escaped.

When I'm sure the connection is severed, I imagine the house struck by a bolt of lightning from the nearing storm. An earth-rattling thunderbolt strikes dead center, and as a blinding light flashes throughout the sky and quickly disappears, the only thing remaining is a house in flames.

Screams shatter the air, drowning out the raging house fire and the howling wind.

I watch for minutes before the screams subside. Satisfied that he is gone, I close my eyes, focusing on the real world and waking up.

Chapter XXXIX

Before I ever open my eyes, I hear the whine of ambulance sirens. I guess that it is for me, and I'm right. The lights above are too bright for me to open my eyes fully, but when I do, I immediately notice the two people sitting on either side of me. I move my head slightly to the right and then back to the left to see who they are. Police officers. I move my hands toward my face to wipe away the sleep, but my hands stop before they reach. The cold of the handcuffs around each wrist pushes deep into my skin as they clank on the metal side rails of the bed I'm lying on. I look down at my leg. The EMT sitting near my head has bandaged it tight to stop as much of the bleeding as possible. The blood, stained through the white gauze wrap and continues to seep through until small drops pool up on the outside.

"What happened?" I ask, looking around for the watch on my wrist. It's gone. The officers must have taken it. I have no way of knowing if this is a dream or not. Neither of the men in the ambulance look in my direction, nor do they acknowledge that I've spoken. I pass out for the remainder of the trip to the hospital. When I regain consciousness, the number of police officers has doubled. One of the officers, a tall, clean-shaven man, stands near my bed with a pad of paper in his left hand. He is clearly a detective, waiting patiently for me to wake.

"Can you tell us what you remember?" he asks without any introduction.

I reach for my head again and again my hand stops short because of the handcuffs on my wrists. The second time the handcuffs clank off the bed rail, a connection suddenly forms in my mind — Hannah must have called the police. Whether or not they have found Waldo's body was anyone's guess. I don't have to wait long to find the answer, however.

"Do you want to tell us about your friend Waldo?" The detective asked in a concerned tone. "Were you going to do the same thing to your friend Hannah?"

I don't answer any of the detective's questions. Instead, I lie still, the events of the last few hours racing through my head. Even if I tell them the truth, the chance of them believing me is slim. Then I remember the handcuffs still strapped to my wrists and every cop movie I've ever seen flashes through my memory.

"I would like to reserve any comments for after I have my attorney present," I say, knowing that I don't have a lawyer. I would most likely be appointed a public defender fifteen minutes before a trial, but I know I don't have to say anything right now. It is hard, though. The only people in the room are cops, and every time I ask for a drink or something to eat, I have the same answer spat back at me.

"We would like to reserve any snacks or beverages for when your attorney is present," a short, balding man says from the corner of the small room.

When I'm stitched up and bandaged, the officers push me in a wheelchair out to a white van waiting in the parking lot. I read the lettering on the side of the van. The message reverberates through my thoughts before hitting me hard in the chest. 'County Jail'.

Chapter XXXX

My cell, small and cold, is occupied by another person. As I sit on my bed on the other side of the room, I try my best not to make eye contact with the man across from me. I introduced myself when I first entered and picked up the man's name, 'Buck', but since then, we haven't said a word to each other. The man named Buck just sits there staring at me for the next hour. He has a large build, weighing nearly three hundred pounds if I had to guess. From the tattoos on his face, neck, and arms, I can tell that Buck enjoys pain. Hopefully, I think, he doesn't enjoy inflicting pain.

I'm wrong.

The first night, I lay awake, fearing sleep for a whole new reason. I can hear the slow, methodical breathing of my cell mate, but I can't tell if he is awake or not. I'm unaware of the time, but I hope that morning will come soon.

Then, it becomes quiet. Too quiet. My ears strain to pick up on Buck's breathing, but it isn't there. All at once, a hand shoots to my chest from the side of my bed, and I'm ripped from my bunk to the floor. The first blow from his fist strikes me in the side of the jaw, making my vision go all fuzzy and my jaw feels like it's now unhinged. Buck is sitting on my chest at this point and my hands are pinned beneath his mammoth legs as if we are children having a tickle fight. I feel helpless, reminding me of the dreams I had no more than three days ago. The next blow finds a landing ground on my nose as I try to lift my head from the ground, sending it back down hard into the cement. The last thing I remember from this night is a heavy blow striking me in the ribs and the sickening crack of bones in my chest.

I'm back in bed when I come to. Both my eyelids are swollen, making it hard to see much. The doctor next to me begins listing my injuries when he sees that I am awake.

"You have three broken ribs, a cracked jaw, a broken nose, and probably a splitting headache from the concussion you suffered. He must not have liked you too much as a roommate," the doctor said, chuckling under his breath.

There is a clock on the wall with large black hands, and while the doctor lists off my injuries, I perform my reality check out of habit. I close my eyes once more in disbelief, taking in a deep breath before coughing and agonizing over my ribs.

All of this is real.

Later that day, my court-appointed lawyer visits me in the infirmary.

"They are going to try to charge you with first degree murder and attempted murder," he says, straightening the tie of his cheap-looking suit.

None of this surprises me. I watched it all happen. The part that I can't wrap my head around is that I will now be going to prison for something another person did. I try to explain this to my attorney but can't get past the first word. It didn't even make sense to me just thinking about it.

"It wasn't me," I finally say, staring directly at my lawyer for the first time. His blue eyes stare straight back at mine, searching for a way to believe me. My lawyer is maybe a little older than me. He looks fresh, not overworked like the state-appointed lawyers I pictured in my head.

"Why don't you tell me what happened?" he says. "Whatever you say is between us. Whether I believe you or not, I will try my best to defend your side of the story."

Chapter XXXXI

I feel safe in the infirmary. And for the first time, I go to sleep unafraid of what waits on the other side of my pillow. With my new freedom in the dream world, I can go where I want and do whatever I wish.

Tonight, however, I'm feeling nostalgic.

I walk through an empty campus, imagining the many conversations shared with friends at the paper. I spend time at the river, throwing a stick for my dog that was taken from me too early. I then walk the few short miles to Waldo's house. We talk for a while about what happened the day before, and he forgives me for getting him killed. It isn't Waldo, but it feels right to apologize and even better to be forgiven.

My last stop, the pink house, comes towards the perceived end of my dream. I have been walking for a long time and hardly notice my feet stop in front of the burned ruin. The house looks like I imagined it would after a fire — black and crumbled.

As I stand there, a familiar voice speaks from behind me. "I didn't think you had it in you," The dream guide says, stepping forward until his shoulders are in line with mine. "But you did it."

He turns toward me, smiling in a way that shows he is both happy for me and deeply sorry. "I'm sorry for the price you had to pay," he said, staring at his shoes now. "No one should ever have to lose a friend that way."

"Yes, such a sad way to lose a friend." A voice echoes from inside the wreckage of the house.

Dream Waldo and I walk toward the house cautiously.

"I know that voice," I think aloud.

As we reach the front porch step, we see a hooded figure in the middle of the rubble, a large piece of mirrored glass piercing the middle of his torso. The glass, which I tried to make unbreakable, is working in a different way; he is unable to use any of his power, and each time he tries to disappear and travel, the mirror only allows half of him to do so. The other half bounces back and forth between the mirror and the floor, causing him to look like a glitch in a game.

"Look," I say, pointing toward him. The hooded man fades in and out like a slowly strobing light. "I think he's getting weaker. He might really be going for good."

"I am going," he says, lying on his back now, giving up any attempts to escape his fate. As his body continues to strobe on and off, I know it's only a matter of moments before he'll be gone forever. Then, he raises his head abruptly. "But I won't be gone."

At these words, Dream Waldo and I look at each other puzzled and back toward the dying man.

"Just think about how many people you've told about me." He smiles a wide, toothy smile. "I'll be visiting them later."

www.ingramcontent.com/pod-product-compliance
Lightning Source LLC
LaVergne TN
LVHW091553060526
838200LV00036B/816
9781800165588